CATCH ME

DANGEROUS ENTANGLEMENTS
BOOK 3

ANNE ROMAN

La Noir Media, LLC

"Here's what I believe, I think the FBI is the premier law enforcement agency in the history of the world but I think there was some bad apples over there."

John Kennedy

CHAPTER ONE

Hannah

They say if you don't learn from your mistakes, you're doomed to repeat them. I had no freaking clue who 'they' were, but as I looked up at the ugly grey building in front of me, I wondered if I was going to end up a victim of the cliche. Just a few weeks ago, I'd stood in the same spot, on the same busy street corner, filled with the self-assurance that I was going to be delivering the hand of justice. Today, though, doubt clouded my thoughts, and I glanced down nervously at my phone for what seemed like the millionth time in the past few hours.

Still nothing.

I could turn around. I could go back to my apartment, smash the burner phone I was clinging to like a desperate hope, and put the entire thing behind me. Sybil had disappeared. No one had seen or heard from her in weeks, and I suspected she'd gone underground when she realized I was closing in on her. They had temporarily lifted my suspension pending a full investigation, but I could still take a leave of absence. I had vacation days to burn. Whatever happens in the secret hearing today could stay there and I could stay out of it. Preferably somewhere in the Bahamas with a mai-thai and endless supply of sunshine.

I heard the engine before I saw it turn down the street and took a step back as a blacked out Triumph motorcycle flew past me. Simon. My heart stuttered. The imaginary taste of rum and coconut soured on my tongue. It wouldn't matter how far I ran, leaving Simon to rot in a prison he didn't deserve to be in was not an option for me.

Reality crashed through me.

I wasn't afraid of the consequences of this hearing or that I would likely lose my job forever. I was afraid of seeing Simon again. Of seeing the accusations in his eyes, or worse. Not seeing anything at all. He'd poured his heart out to me in Helsinki. Shared all his fears and regrets over how he'd treated me, only for me to turn around and betray them all. I didn't know if I'd be able to forgive myself, either. But I would do this. I would look him in the eye and take whatever he offered. And then he could disappear from my life and into the shadows where he belonged, like the Ghost he was. Only to haunt me forever.

————

I was back in a conference room and I realized I would be perfectly happy if I never saw the inside of a room like this again. Agent Reed sat to my left, shuffling a stack of papers and clearing his throat just about every thirty seconds. I bit the inside of my cheek and tried to keep my eyes trained on the door as we waited for everyone else to arrive. He cleared it again, and I tasted blood.

"Cough drop?" I reached in my purse and pulled out a wrapped cherry flavored drop, sliding it towards him. He looked down at it and then looked back up as he pushed his glasses further up his nose, giving me a blank stare.

"No, thank you Agent Kelly." And then he cleared his throat again and went back to reading through the papers in front of him. I huffed and squirmed in my seat. Most of the courthouse was empty. It was after hours and all the cases on the dockets for the day were done. The only people left in the building were the janitors, the security guards, and us.

The quiet of the room and the heavy emptiness of the building seemed to press down on me. Agent Reed chuffed again, and I picked up the cough drop, slamming it on the stack of papers in front of him. "No really, I insist."

Watery brown eyes turned towards me, widening at my outburst before he slowly reached out and picked it up, twirling it through his fingers. "You seem a little stressed, Agent Kelly. Is every-thing alright?" The question was innocent enough, but his voice was filled with an underlying venom. I shifted in my seat and turned away, my eyes returning to stare at the door. "Nope, just looking out for my fellow agent, Agent Reed."

Out of the corner of my eye, I could see his lips twitch and he leaned forward. I could smell the scent of coffee and cheap aftershave. "I heard that about you Agent Kelly, that you like to look out for your fellow Agents." He tapped the cough drop on the back of my hand, where I had placed it on the table, gripping the wrapped end and drawing a slow line from my finger up to my wrist. Then he turned my palm over, placing the drop in the very center, before closing my fingers over it. "I like to look out for my Agents too. Maybe when this is over, we can look out for each other." He cleared his throat and went back to reading his papers. Bile rose and visions of shoving the cough drop down his throat to choke on it danced through my head.

Just as I was opening my mouth to respond, the conference room door swung open and two federal security officers walked in, followed by a face that made my mouth go dry while other parts of me did the exact opposite. I sat forward a little more and watched as he entered, eager to drink in the sight of him. This was the second time I'd seen him in a prison jumpsuit. Only this time, he wasn't half covered in blood. Stormy grey eyes found mine and for the second time this evening, my heart stuttered. If he was shocked or felt any emotions at all, he didn't betray them. I tried to keep my features just as blank. A guard approached and Simon held out his hands as they removed the handcuffs before they led him to a seat placed just off the conference table. The arms of the seat held bolts that they looped his chains back through, and the cuffs were once again locked back into place.

Simon didn't even look at the guards, who were busy re-securing him. He kept his stony gaze locked with mine. "A bit of an overkill, don't you think?" I thought for a moment he was asking me the question and was about to agree with him, but then he shifted his focus to Agent Reed. The way he dismissed me stung, and I tried to ignore how my heart sank. I knew seeing Simon was going to be difficult and that he would not be pleased to see me. But a small part of me had hoped that maybe he'd realized what I'd done was to protect him. That I wasn't given much of a choice and had made the best out of a crappy situation.

Agent Reed cleared his throat again. "I've learned not to let my guard down around you, Mr. Gallagher. You have an unnatural ability to suddenly disappear. And when that happens, someone inevitably ends up injured or dead." His eyes narrowed, and I noticed Reed had unconsciously brought his hand up to massage a spot on his throat. It was then that I noticed a faint scar, and I looked from Reed to Simon, curious about the exchange I was witnessing. Simon seemed to catch the motion as well, and a sinister smirk curled at his full lips. "How's your throat Frank? I never got a chance to apologize for that."

Reed dropped his hand quickly and glared. "I have permanent scar tissue damage and I can't eat or drink without pain." A mocking smile appeared. "But don't worry, I'm in excellent hands. The bureau looks out for its agents, doesn't it, Agent Kelly?" His oily voice curled around my ears and I turned to him, glaring. But I could see it, the challenge in his eyes as he dared me to speak up against him. I swallowed around the words I wanted to say and nodded. "Yes, Agent Reed. The bureau takes care of their agents." I glanced back at Simon as I spoke and faltered. His grey eyes were piercing through me with an intensity that was full of dark promises, and I felt my body heat in response. "We always look out for our own." It felt like my words came out in a whisper, but I knew he heard them. I just prayed he understood.

The guards moved to step away from Simon, taking up positions behind him and then the door to the conference room opened once more to allow Agent Waters to enter and I felt a bit of the tension in my shoulders ease. She took a seat across the table from us just as a second door, leading from what I presumed were the Judge's chambers, opened and a disgruntled-looking man in his late fifties or early sixties entered. A frazzled-looking bailiff hurried after him and gave a half-hearted "All Rise..." before the judge waved a hand in his face. "Enough of that. It's late. Let's just get on with this."

We all paused, half-way out of our seats as the judge took his own chair at the head of the table and grabbed a gavel, giving it two knocks on the table. "Alright, let's get this over with. What's the charges?"

My stomach turned. It was now or never. My hand rose to grip the Saint Michael's pendant around my neck. Please let this work.

CHAPTER TWO

Hannah

Agent Reed held up a manila envelope for the Bailiff to collect and gave the judge a charming smile. "Your Honor, thank you for attending this matter on such short notice. Mr. Gallagher has been a known target of the bureau for some time now. We're requesting that given his connections with foreign governments and the depth of his resources, he be moved to a maximum security prison in an undisclosed location until he can await a full trial."

I sat up at the words 'undisclosed location. "You're talking about a CIA black site." My outburst caused everyone at the table to turn towards me, but my eyes were locked onto Simon, whose only reaction was to remain coldly indifferent. Fear squeezed my heart. If Simon was sent to a black site, it wasn't to detain him. It was to kill him. I knew Simon had connections and more than a grey area in his past. But to want him put to death? Ice-cold fear flooded my veins.

Reed cocked his head slightly. "Yes, Agent Kelly, you are correct. Mr. Gallagher's reputation and his resources are of a particular interest to the Agency." He turned back to the judge and dismissed me. "As you can see, your Honor, we have the authority to request his release and transfer. We are in full cooperation with the Agency."

The judge looked from me to Agent Reed and then back down to the file in his hands. "And you're certain you have the authority necessary to request this transfer? Or that I have the authority to grant it?" He frowned, reading through the file, and flipped over a page.

"We are certain of it, Your Honor." Reed's smile could have cut diamonds, and I wanted to scream "Liar!" Very limited federal authority could grant the transfer that Reed was suggesting. He was either lying through his teeth or had managed to bribe someone very high up in the State Department to give him the leeway. This wasn't a hearing to determine charges or set bail. This was a witch hunt. But I had no proof and as much as it killed me, I had to wait to see how everything played out.

"Very well then. I see no rea- "A loud knock interrupted the judge's statement, and we all turned towards the conference room door. The bailiff, frowning, moved to open it and I could just hear the hushed undertones of a conversation before the door was shut. He returned to the judge's side, where he leaned down and whispered in his ear before handing him a sheet of paper.

The judge frowned, and his eyes scanned the text before nodding. "Agent Reed, I'm afraid we're going to have to postpone this discussion."

Reed's face grew red, and he sputtered. "What do you mean, Your Honor? I don't understand. This matter is of the highest urgency."

The judge nodded. "Oh, I agree. This is absolutely of the highest urgency. However, it seems Mr. Gallagher is a popular man and the memorandum that I've just received has tied my hands." The judge turned to the guards. "You may release him."

Reed stood up and slammed his hands down on the table. "I want to see that memorandum. Who the hell has the authority to release a man in federal custody?"

Just then, the door opened, and a tall man in a crisp military uniform entered. He was striking, with sharp cheekbones, just the hint of graying hair around his temples, and an intensity in his gaze that made goosebumps dance across my skin. Thankfully, that gaze was locked on Agent Reed and he answered him with a voice that commanded the room. "The Secretary of State and Secretary of Defense do."

The judge stood up and cleared his throat. "Sir, I'd appreciate it if you did not interrupt my court room or proceedings."

The man nodded. "My apologies, Your Honor. My name is Colonel Jonathan Abrams. I have orders to ensure that the instructions in that memo are followed to the letter." He dropped his gaze back down to Agent Reed, who still had his mouth gaped open like a fish. "And to make sure it was understood, in no uncertain terms, that Mr. Gallagher has the full backing and support of the State Department and the Pentagon." Glee filled me and I couldn't help the grin that broke out across my face, only to fall when that piercing gaze was turned onto me and, with a pointed stare, said. "For now."

Reed spoke up again, apparently not content to let his prize slip through his hands. "You'll have to forgive me, Colonel, was it? But I have no clue who you are or what authority you think you can operate here. This is a federal criminal matter."

Agent Waters spoke up then, her voice winding through the tension in the room like smoke. "Apparently, Frank, it's a state department matter now." The entire time we'd been in the conference room, Agent Waters had remained so still and silent I'd nearly forgotten her presence. But now that her voice curled around us in a raspy whisper, I felt my palms grow sweaty with nervousness again. "But it seems there is another matter to discuss." She turned towards me. "Would you care to enlighten the room on why I'm here, Agent Kelly?"

I swallowed past the lump in my throat and nodded. It was show time. "Yes, Agent Waters," I turned towards the judge and withdrew another plain manilla envelope I'd been hiding under the table before offering it to the bailiff. "Your Honor, there is another matter of federal importance that we need you to sign off on."

The judge frowned. "This is a highly unusual procedure, Agent Kelly. Are you sure this isn't a matter for a lower court?"

I offered the judge a smile. "Yes, Your Honor. The request was submitted and approved just before we arrived this evening."

He glanced up from what he was reading, shock in his expression. "This is a request for a search and seizure of government property and a warrant for the arrest of a federal investigator. For you, Agent Reed."

It took everything I had to maintain my composure as I watched Reed turn multiple shades of red and purple as he whirled towards me. "Is this some sort of sick joke?" Rage made his voice shake. "Just what kind of game are you playing at, Agent Kelly? May I remind you that your career is on the line here? And yet you think you're going to have some sort of coup de grâce over me?"

He was mere inches from my face, and I could feel his hot breath wash over me. Gross.

"No Agent Reed, I would never consider the torture and abuse of a minor a laughing matter." Shock and a glimmer of fear replaced rage.

"I have no clue what you're inferring Kelly, but you had better pray to god that whatever game you're trying to play doesn't backfire because I can assure you, you will have nothing left to come back to at any level of the bureau when I'm done with you."

I smirked and sat back in my chair, crossing my arms. "Agent Reed, are you threatening me?"

He stood suddenly and started towards me, but must have thought better about it and stepped back with a snarl before turning to Agent Waters. "Angela, this is ridiculous. I don't know what Agent Kelly thinks she has on me, but I assure you, it's nothing more than a twisted ploy to keep her in her position. I have done nothing wrong."

I took the momentary lapse in Reed's scrutiny of me to glance around the room, noticing how still and silent Simon sat as he watched the exchange. The only evidence of his thoughts was a small frown of confusion on his face. When he finally noticed me looking at him, he arched one eyebrow in question. It was the first time he'd really acknowledged me since he'd walked into the room, and I felt my heart leap with hope. He'd worked it out then. Now I just needed him to trust me to see it finished.

When I tuned back into the conversation, Agent Waters was speaking. "Do you remember a case you worked as a field agent about 10 years ago, Agent Reed? A case involving cyber theft?"

Reed shook his head. "I've worked dozens of cases Angela, you're going to have to be more specific than that. And if you're saying this is all based on the word of some low life I've put away, I think we both know how much weight their words will hold against mine."

I pulled another file from my purse and slapped

it down on the table, the little audience in the room turning back towards me. "Oh, this is actually one 'low life' that you never had the chance to put away. Probably because," I held up one finger. "One, they weren't a low life to begin with and two," I flipped open the file to the face of a young girl, hair pulled back into twin pigtails and amber-colored eyes that were wide, scared, and haunted. ", she was a minor. A minor that you held without justification and subjected to torturous conditions and interrogations for days."

Reed had the decency to pale in front of me. His Adams apple bobbed as he swallowed before he reached out to snatch the file away from me. I pulled it back and clicked my tongue at him. "Oh no, no Agent Reed, you know better. You're going to have to ask your lawyer to file a request for this evidence if you want to look at it before your grand jury date."

He snarled. "Those files were confidential and restricted. How did you steal them?"

I rolled my eyes. "Oh, please Reed. How long did you think someone was going to cover for you? You've made a lot of enemies on your way to the top. Turns out once I had the witnesses' testimony, it wasn't hard to narrow down just who the agent in charge of that case was. And from there, it was only a matter of getting the files unsealed and on the appropriate desks." I cocked my head and smiled. "Turns out the bureau does indeed take reports of misconduct by its agents very seriously."

Agent Waters stood up and moved around me to stand in front of Reed. "Agent Frank Reed, you're under arrest for the misconduct relating to a federal agent and the inappropriate exploitation and interrogation of a minor." Her voice trailed off as Frank sputtered and coughed, but I wasn't watching him anymore because my eyes were on Simon. The guards had finally released him and he was standing next to Colonel Abrams, their heads bent towards each other, but their words were too muffled by Reed's screeching for me to hear what they were saying. As if they both felt eyes on them, each one looked up and turned towards me at the same time and I shivered under the intensity of their gaze. These were two men who should probably never be in the same room together or meet on the opposite sides of a war. I pitied anyone who ended up caught in the crossfire. Then Simon nodded toward me, just once, before moving to the door, the Colonel following closely behind him. I didn't even have a chance to stand up and go after him. The door closed with a click and just like that, Simon Gallagher disappeared. Again.

CHAPTER THREE

Hannah

"Chunky Monkey or Moose Tracks?"

Cold blasted me from the open freezer door as I contemplated the two choices. "Oh, I don't know Hannah, which coma-inducing ice-cream screams 'drowning my sorrows in chocolate' the loudest?"

Was I standing in front of my refrigerator talking to myself about ice-cream choices and feeling completely sorry for myself about the shitty way my life had been going lately? Yes, yes, I was. I frowned, glaring at the smiling faces of two animals on frozen cartons, trying to sell me false happiness in the form of diabetes. "Fine, Chunky Monkey it is. Not a fan of moose, anyway."

Grabbing the carton, I slammed the freezer door closed before turning to my rack of dishes and fished around for a clean spoon. I didn't have any need for a bowl. It was just going to be me, this spoon, and a broken heart for the rest of the evening. I'd told myself that tonight I would console myself with wine and chocolate. But that tomorrow I would move on with my head held high, knowing I did the right thing. By now, Simon should be back with his team, assuming that the word of Agent Waters was good, and they would be off on whatever mission they were assigned to next. And I would be here in my dinky apartment, with no job and definitely no secret mission. Just me, my books, and Mr. Chunky Monkey. I flopped down on my couch and stared at the smiling monkey holding his banana and riding a wave of chocolate and walnuts. "Probably going to be just me and you for a long time Mr. Chunk." I mock "cheered" him with the back of my spoon. "Here's to a long lasting whatever this is."

My phone buzzed on the coffee table, and I set the carton down with a sigh as I reached for it and swiped the screen open.

Unknown Number: Chunky Monkey won't solve all your problems.

I froze. One hand still holding my spoon and the other holding my phone as all my senses went on high alert.

Unknown Number: And now you're thinking that someone is watching you, but I assure you, I am not.

Unknown Number: I just know you better than you know yourself.

I set the spoon down slowly and then texted back.

Me: Funny, I'm pretty sure I know myself very damn well, because Chunky Monkey has always solved my problems.

Unknown Number: Wrong, Hannah. Chunky Monkey is a distraction. You run to distractions when the truth is too overwhelming for you to handle.

Unknown Number: Like the fact that you are currently sitting in your crappy apartment with a career down the drain, in love with a man who could never allow himself to form attachments, all while being hunted by an underground criminal group that is very upset with how much you've disrupted their status quo.

I swallowed, a pit forming in my stomach, and my hands shook as I responded.

Me: Very cute Sybil. Why don't you come by and tell me all about my miserable life in person? It's your favorite game.

Unknown Number: Finally, putting your brain

to work. Good job, but not good enough. You're being hunted, Hannah, and you don't even realize it.

Me: If you're trying to scare me, Sis, that train has passed. I'm not afraid of your royal pain in everyone's ass anymore.

Unknown Number: Still as obtuse as ever. This is the only warning you will get. You've ruffled quite a few feathers.

Me: I thought you would be glad someone else is hunting me. Isn't that what you wanted? Me gone and out of your way?

I stared at my phone, waiting for her response, but it never came. Chunky Monkey sat forgotten on my table, the carton dripping melted chocolate onto the faux wood top. When I realized those little text bubbles weren't going to pop back up, I picked up the ice-cream and spoon, stomped over to my kitchen and hurled them into the trash.

"Did the spoon deserve that..." I whirled, my Glock 19 out of the waistband of my yoga pants and in my hand. My thumb was instantly on the safety, ready to switch it off, as I aimed at the head of the voice that growled behind me.

"... lass?" Steel-grey eyes glinted in the low lighting of my living room and I stood there, speechless.

He moved closer, gaze flicking down to my gun and then back up at me as a smirk curled the corners of his lips. "This is the third, or is it the fourth, time you've pointed your weapon at me? Are you ever going to pull the trigger?"

Somehow I found my voice. "I might. Depends on if you keep calling me lass or not." My hand lowered, and I moved the thumb off the safety. He was here, in my apartment, and he hadn't disappeared into the shadows like I'd thought he would. Like he should have. Why?

Simon towered over me, his body blocking out the light from the soft lamp that lit my living room. I wanted to back away. I wanted to see all of him, to blink and make sure my heart wasn't imagining things, but all I could do was tilt my head back and stare.

He reached out, fingers tracing my jaw, my neck, leaving a burning trail across my skin until they slowly slid down the length of my arm to where my hand still gripped my gun.

"I think we both know that's never going to happen." He pried the weapon gently from my fingers and I let him. His earthy scent washed over me, filling my senses. He smelled like pine and leather. I wanted to wrap myself in it and never let it go.

"What's not going to happen?" My voice was husky as I responded. "I'm not going to shoot you? Or you're not going to stop calling me lass."

He moved in even closer, his body brushing against mine as he reached around me to lay the gun on the counter that was just behind me.

"Both."

Then he tipped up my chin, the pad of his thumb brushing against my bottom lip. "You got me captured."

There was no malice or question in his voice. It was a simple statement of fact. I tried to think around the sensation of his thumb dragging slowly over my lip, his other hand finding its way under the edge of my t-shirt to curl against my waist, pinning me to him. I didn't realize he was moving me away from my kitchen until I felt the press of wood from my bookshelves against my back.

"I did."

His body radiated heat, but everywhere he touched, my skin pebbled. It felt like I was trapped in a spell he was creating and when he leaned down to run his lips against the side of my jaw and down my neck, all of my nerve endings suddenly came alive. I let my head fall back against the shelves, giving him more access.

His lips moved against my skin, teeth barely

grazing the sensitive area between my neck and collarbone. "And then you risked yourself to get me free." He paused, pulling away, and my eyes flew open in protest at the loss of contact. "Again." There was a glint in the depth of his gaze that made my heart race. It was the same dark look he'd given me in the courtroom.

I frowned and tried to control the pounding of my heart and the flood of desire he'd ignited with just a few touches. "I had a plan."

One dark brow arched in a look I was becoming familiar with. "Aye, that you did." He stepped back in close to me again, both his hands coming up to cup my face. "And it was brilliant. Thank you, Hannah."

I was speechless again. Had Simon Gallagher just thanked me? A small smile played on his lips, as if he could read my thoughts. "Aye, lass, thank you. But not for what you think. Thank you for Rue. For what you did for her. It was something, even with all my connections, I could never get done." He frowned then, suddenly serious. "But the other part? Calling in Abrams? Risking your career that way? You didn't have to do that. I would have eventually been released."

I shook my head, "Abrams was Michaels idea. And I'm glad I did it. Didn't you hear Reed? They wanted to send you to an Agency black site, Simon." My hands came up to grip the leather collar of his jacket as I tried not to let the fear of him being sent to a place like that overwhelm me. "I couldn't let that happen. You don't deserve that."

He leaned down, his forehead pressing to mine, and my heart flipped inside my chest. "Hannah, love, don't you think I've had my fair share of experience in a place like that? I told you, this is my world and I understand the risks in every choice I make. But I did not mean you to be a part of this."

I breathed him in. "What if I wanted to be?" He stilled and pulled away to look down at me, his eyes searching mine.

"Do you want to be?" He didn't give away anything in his words or his gaze.

Did I? A big part of me screamed yes. The part of me that had never wanted to settle in one place. The part of me that craved the rush, the chaos, and ultimately, freedom. The part that relished seeing monsters like my sister and Sergei brought to justice. But the other part of me knew what he was asking. To step away from this life meant disconnecting from everything, and everyone, I knew. And then there was the bigger question I needed to answer. Did I want this because of the man standing in front of me? Or did I want it for myself?

CHAPTER FOUR

Simon

"What if I wanted to be?"

Just like every time I was near Hannah, all my self-control went out the window and I was at the mercy of the vixen in front of me. She'd hurled the ice cream in the trash and I'd immediately wanted to strip her naked and take her there on the kitchen floor. To have her writhing in pleasure beneath me until she'd let go of the fear, anger, and sadness. In the cries of her release and the taste of it on my tongue and fingers.

Then she'd pointed her gun at me, again, and any shred of hope I'd had of just thanking her and leaving had gone up in smoke. Who was I kidding? Hannah drew me in like a moth to a flame. I'd spent hours trying to convince myself it was best just to disappear and leave the country. We'd already received our next assignment, no thanks to Colonel Abrams, and Michael and Rue were en route to link up with me. I'd told myself it was better for Hannah and for me to accept this for what it was and to let her go, even while I was speeding down the highway to her apartment. Even while I was slipping the key I'd had made into her door when she hadn't heard me knock. Even as I was standing in front of her, drowning in the emerald green color of her eyes. I was a fool.

"Do you want to be?"

Her question lit something inside of me I thought had died out a long time ago. Hope flared, and it took every effort to push it back down into the dark depths of my heart. I didn't want her involved in this messy business, not because I didn't think she couldn't handle it, or because of some misogynistic idea that she shouldn't be in my line of work. No, if anything, I'd thought time and time again that Hannah was born for this life. Her actions in Estonia and the way she'd tracked down Sergei proved she was more than capable. But it had to be her choice.

I'd taken that choice away when I'd tricked her

into being my asset and bait. Sybil had taken away her choice when she'd manipulated her into staying with the bureau in Atlanta. Even her boss had taken away her choice when he'd forced her to betray us in order to satisfy his own vendetta against me. I watched as indecision warred across her face and knew the answer to my question, but didn't wait for her response. Hope was a delicate thing to crush, and I didn't know if my heart could handle hearing her say it out loud.

Instead, my lips found hers, and I growled at her little gasp of surprise. "Never mind. Tell me how you figured out that Reed was the one who had been assigned to Rue's case. I never told you."

I couldn't stop touching her and with every caress of her soft skin under the palm of my hands, the need to rip her yoga pants off her body burned through me. The woman should be banned from ever wearing yoga pants in my presence. She rocked her hips into mine and moaned as my fingers found their way from her ribcage to cup her breast, skimming across a nipple. No bra. She was going to be the death of me.

"It wasn't hard." Her casual confidence made me smirk against the skin of her exposed shoulder where I was placing soft kisses, tasting her.

"Not hard? I've spent years trying to get those files unsealed. You did it in a matter of days." I sucked in a breath as her hands wandered under my shirt, tracing a path down to the waistband of my pants where they dropped lower, and she palmed my hardness through my jeans. "Careful, lass." I growled into her ear. "You're not going to distract me from getting the information I want."

"Is that what this is?" She turned her face towards me and caught my bottom lip in her teeth, biting down with just enough force to sting. "Am I being interrogated now, Mr. Gallagher?" Humor laced the huskiness in her voice.

"No, love, if I was interrogating you, you'd be screaming by now." To prove my point, I slipped one hand between her thighs, feeling the wetness that pooled between them and pressed against her sweet spot hidden by the thin fabric of her pants. I was rewarded with a whimper of pleasure, her body rocking against my hand on its own. "Now, are you going to tell me? Or do I have to get more inventive with my techniques?"

She moaned, her hips rolling against my fingers as I continued to apply pressure against the sensitive nerves, but didn't move them to give her the relief she wanted. "I don't like games, Simon."

"Too bad. Looks like I need to be more direct

in my tactics." I dropped to my knees, removing my hand from between her thighs, hooking my thumbs into the waistband of her pants and rolling them down her hips. Once I had a leg free, I hooked it over my shoulder and leaned in, breathing in her intoxicating scent, and zeroed in on the sight of her swollen and dripping for me. I looked up. She was staring, her face flushed, eyes glazed and her kiss-swollen, lips parted with desire. "Last warning, love. Are you going to give me the information I need?"

A mischievous smirk twisted her lips and flashed in her eyes. She moved her hand down to her glistening core and pulled back the folds, exposing her clit and creamy channel. "Do your worst."

Need slammed through me, the part of my brain that defined me as a man going dark. This was no longer a game, this was a claiming. My tongue lashed at her pussy, teeth grazing her sensitive nub and not stopping at the hiss of pain or the rake of nails on my scalp. Because even as I devoured her like some sort of beast, her juices were flooding my mouth, her body shaking.

I pulled back just enough to speak, tongue circling her swollen nub tenderly. "Should I continue? Or are you ready to talk?"

"Si..." She was panting, her knees shaking, but I didn't let her get any other words out.

"Have it your way." And then I attacked her greedy pussy again, my tongue filling her as deep as I could go before drawing back and replacing it with two fingers. With her wetness still coating my face, I stood up, fingers driving into her with a steady rhythm, and captured her lips with mine.

"Do you taste yerself, lass? Do you taste how sweet you are?"

I felt her response on my fingers as she quivered and clenched around them. Her core milked my fingers as her release tore through her body. I could have stayed there all night teasing every ounce of pleasure from her. But I withdrew to a low whimper of displeasure as I'd spied something behind her on the shelf and an idea began to take form.

I was rewarded with a pouty glare as I pulled away. "Are you done interrogating me already? I thought you were supposed to be a professional at this." The frustration and bratty tone made me grin even more as I reached for the book I'd skimmed through the first time I'd visited her in the apartment.

"I'm merely adjusting my techniques. You're a special case, lass." I held up the book and watched as confusion and then apprehension washed over her features.

"What do you intend to do with my book? I swear if you do anything to ruin it, I will shoot you."

I grinned. "Well now, you just gave away a bargaining chip. We really need to work on your negotiating techniques." She opened her mouth to speak, but I interrupted her. "For every truth you tell me, I will make one of your fantasies from this book come true." Her eyes widened as she looked from the book I was holding and then back to me, a blush creeping up her cheeks.

I flipped through the pages and arched a brow. "Looks like chapter 55 has seen quite a bit of wear and tear. Favorite chapter?" Her mouth snapped shut, and she glared.

"I can't tell if you're being serious or teasing me, so I'm not inclined to accept your proposal. But I'll still shoot you if you ruin that book." She reached out to grab it out of my hands, but I held it aloft and shook my head.

"This isn't a joke, lass. I know how much you love your fantasies. Let me fulfill them." I didn't add that I wanted to be her fantasy. To be the one that made them come true and also inspired them. That was something that I couldn't promise her, though. But this, this I could give. I just hoped that when it was time to walk away for good, it would be enough. For the both of us. "All you have to do is tell me the truth."

She stared at me for a long second, seeming to assess my seriousness, and then glanced back to the book and nodded slowly. "Fine, but I have conditions. I get to pick scenes from different books. I like that chapter, but if I'm going to get some fantasies fulfilled, I think I should get to pick which ones they are."

I grinned. "Fair. One scene from any book you choose for every question you answer."

"And," she held up one finger, and I arched a brow at her. "You also have to answer my questions. Truthfully."

"You already stated your condition, princess." I shook my head. "Now you're just being greedy."

"Wrong. I said 'conditions', plural. And I don't think this is being greedy. You're going to get double the reward, my fantasies and my answers. I think it's only fair that I get the same thing in return." She cocked her head, her eyes wide and innocent but sparkling with the knowledge that she'd thrown my words back in my face. "How's that for negotiating?"

I swallowed thickly, suddenly unsure of the

game I'd started, but nodded slowly. "Very good. I agree with your conditions." I let my gaze drag down her body, devouring and mapping every sexy inch and then slowly back up to where she was staring at me with lust filled eyes again.

"Shall we begin?"

CHAPTER FIVE

Hannah

This was an intimacy I'd been unprepared to deal with. For a long time, books had been my only escape from the hell I'd felt trapped in. When Sybil had alienated me from my friends, I'd clung to the words, the worlds, and the friendships I'd found in them. The more attached to Sybil's hip I was, the more withdrawn into faraway romances and adventures I'd become.

The only time I'd really taken a break in my reading hobby had been while I was attending a local state college and Sybil had been away at Georgia Tech. Then, I'd made a few friends in my law classes and had even reconnected with some of my old highschool friends. But every time Sybil came home, they didn't exist anymore. Then, once I'd graduated and started applying for jobs with the FBI, Sybil had insinuated that she was too scared and lonely to be in Atlanta by herself. So I'd packed my books up and moved to the city I now called home.

Simon stepped away, and I dragged my pants back on. Was I a little disgruntled that this new game he was playing had interrupted our fun? Maybe. But curiosity was getting the better of me and I'd conceded just to see where this would go. This was my chance to get some honest answers from the elusive Ghost and I would not let it go to waste.

His eyes were still dark with desire as he tracked the movements of my pants sliding over my hips and for a moment, I thought he was going to tell me to stop. But then he just grinned and sat down on my couch, one leg crossing over his knee with the casualness of male arrogance.

"I'm not sure what I like better, you in those pants, or out of them."

I shook my head, unable to resist an answering grin. "Well, considering how I seem to end up out of them every time you come around, I'd say the latter." I held out my hand. "Book please."

He seemed to hesitate for a moment before carefully placing it in my hand, where I then turned to carefully return it to its proper place on my shelf. My life may have been in disarray, but I was nearly OCD about my bookshelves and each book had its correct placement according to genre, author, and sometimes even color. When I was done, I moved to sit down on the couch next to him.

"So," I cocked my head and studied him, suddenly unsure of what the next steps would be. We'd made a bargain. But how that bargain would play out remained to be seen. "Who goes first?"

He studied me for a moment in the same manner, as if he, too, was just realizing the weight of the agreement we'd made. For every truth I told, he had to tell one as well. The fantasy fulfillment was just the sweetener to bind the deal. But to get the reward, we were both going to do something we'd never done until this point with each other. Be honest.

He cleared his throat and sat forward. "Well, since it's my bargain, I suppose it should be me. How did you figure out Reed was the agent who interrogated Rue?"

Relief and disappointment filled me at the same time as part of me was thankful that he'd asked such a softball question and the other part of me wished he'd asked the question I really wanted to answer.

"When Rue told me her story in Stockholm, I remembered reading reports and case studies that mentioned a few of the agents in charge of the Fleur de Lis case. Reed's name stuck out. I couldn't figure out how he'd gotten away with it, though. No one with that kind of history would have made it to the level he is at, or was at, now." I scooted back into the sofa and drew my legs towards my chest, my arms coming to wrap around my knees. "That's when I realized no one actually knew the age or the description of the Fleur de lis. They were really good about never mentioning any specific details and we all just assumed it was an adult. So I figured any files from then hadn't been updated yet to the new system." For several years now, the FBI had been working to digitize all files and cases into one central electronic filing system. All but a few had been cataloged. "I called in a favor to see if there were any files in Agent Reed's past case log that hadn't been uploaded yet. Low and behold, there were quite a few that seemed to be missing from the new system. My friend requested to see those files and suddenly there were a lot of questions about why they were omitted." I shrugged slightly. "And from there, it just snowballed. They found the files, unsealed them and then delivered them to the desks that needed to see them." Simon listened to me with eyes sparkling with intense interest, never interrupting to ask questions or admonish me or my methods. "It seems your friend Frank had quite a few cases he was hoping wouldn't make it to the new system. He didn't want anyone to have a permanent record of his indiscretions."

Suddenly Simon moved in, so fast I barely registered he was moving, and kissed me. It was slow, soft and lingering. So different from the other kisses he had given me. I melted into him as a new kind of heat blazed, lighting me from within. And when he pulled away, I had to resist the urge to follow, seeking more.

My lips stayed parted, "I hope you don't think that was you fulfilling your part of the bargain."

He smirked, "No lass, that was me saying that you're brilliant. But I'm pretty sure a knock- your- socks off kind of kiss is in one of your fantasies."

I blushed. I didn't want to admit that a world ending kiss actually was on my list. "If that was a fantasy kiss, you have some studying to do. But don't worry, I'll get you caught up." I waved a hand, dismissing him and hoping that he couldn't see the effect his kiss had on me. The smirk I ignored told me he knew exactly how much it did. I continued on, "Well, hopefully my brilliance pays off, and Rue knows I'm truly sorry for what I had to do." Part of me worried that I'd done permanent damage to the budding friendship I'd developed with the beautiful hacker and mercenary. Simon seemed to read my thoughts and grabbed my hand, giving it a gentle squeeze.

"Rue is tough, Hannah. She's also one of the most loyal people I've ever met. She was more pissed that you managed to get the drop on her than anything. When she finds out what you did for her, there won't be anything left to forgive."

Some of the worry faded away, and I smiled, giving his hand a squeeze in return. "Alright, my turn then." I watched as some of the wariness returned in his gaze, but he didn't let go of my hand, just nodded and said, "Ok, your turn."

My eyes traced over every angle and plane of his face, noting the shadow of a dark beard coming in on his jaw and the way his gun metal colored eyes glinted in the low lamp lighting. Finally, I unlodged my tongue and asked the question that had been swirling around since he'd left me in Stockholm.

"What's my sister's connection to Tory?"

One blink was all that he gave me to show that my question had startled him and for a moment he was so still that I thought he wasn't going to answer. I started to pull my hand away, but he gripped it tighter, his thumb beginning to slowly trace over my wrist and the pulse that fluttered there.

"That's," he hesitated. "A complicated question."

I cocked my head, eyes narrowing. "We made a deal." But I didn't pull my hand back any further.

"I know, and I want to give you an answer, but it's going to take more time than we've got right now."

"Then give me the cliff notes version." I waited to see if he would run from the question, or face me and give me the honesty I needed.

"You know, the Abromov group recruited Sybil as part of their effort to gain tech secrets, as well as bring brilliant minds into their organization." I nodded. Technological theft from foreign espionage was nothing new and Sybil's connection to the research department at Georgia Tech would have provided her with ample access to innovative programs and developments.

"Well, another part of their recruitment efforts went to indoctrinate disgruntled patriots who may be looking for an outlet for their frustrations. They use back channels, social media chats, or online groups to reach them. That's how Sybil got her claws into Tory." He cleared his throat and let go of my hand, leaning forward to brace his arms on his knees. I adjusted to scoot closer to him, but like he did with me, didn't interrupt, just waited for him to continue.

"Tory was angry and tired of the," he frowned at the memory, clearly bothered by it. "... restrictions, our government placed on us when we were on a mission. This was before we'd pulled away and operated as a complete Ghost unit. Before that, we were still technically a part of the British Military. She hated the pay. She hated the time away." He shook his head. "I thought she was just ready to get out. Get married, settle down. I thought if I could just convince her to stick it out for a few more rotations, we could be completely done. Off the books and done." He looked at me then. "Do you know why I hated Sybil so much, lass? It wasn't because she took Tory from me. It was because she knew her better than I did."

I frowned. "So you're saying that Tory was radicalized in a chatroom?"

He nodded, his fists clenching and unclenching. "Who knows? Maybe she was already that way and I just didn't realize it. I knew she liked to vent her frustrations and sometimes would say things that were kind of crazy, but I always brushed her off as just being unhappy. Somehow word got to the

Abromov group and I'm sure it didn't take them long to figure out who Tory was or what she did in the military. To be honest, I'm not entirely sure she didn't seek them out herself. That's when Sybil showed up."

He ran fingers through his dark hair and he glared at the floor, a sudden edginess taking over him. "To put it simply, Tory sold us out. She knew from Sybil that the same weapons dealers we'd been chasing in Syria were the same buyers that the Abromov group had lined up. She tipped them off and was expecting a big payday from it. But then Sybil betrayed her, and when we showed up, there was an ambush waiting. Tory was caught in the crossfire." The words tumbled out of him, dark and angry. "When she realized Sybil wasn't going to rescue her, she thought she'd get some bonus points with the militants if she took out our team. Michael and Evan were with me. She used some of the weapons and set a trap, intending to blow us up and make it look like an IED went off. I caught her with the detonator switch." He swiveled his gaze towards me and there was no remorse, no guilt, in those dark eyes. 'I killed her."

CHAPTER SIX

Hannah

Turning away, he blinked at the blank space in front of him as if by doing so he could remove the memory that played out in the theatre of his mind, then turned those delicious dark greys towards me. There was none of the sadness or regret that I expected to see in them. Just the clear-eyed gaze of a man who had made a hard choice but fully understood and accepted the consequences.

"And you've been hunting my sister ever since." It wasn't a question, but a statement, and he nodded slowly in confirmation.

"Aye. At first it was because I'd convinced myself that the militants and terrorists cells we hunted were just the little fish. I wanted the big fish. The Abromov group and everyone they associated with. But in reality, it was all about revenge. I blamed Sybil for Tory's choices and beliefs." He settled back into the couch as if the weight of his confession were suddenly lifted and he could relax. "It wasn't until recently that I stopped lying to myself and admitted the truth."

My head dropped to my knees, still tucked against my body as I studied him. A relaxed Simon was something new. The way he took up space on my couch, in my life, was always so imposing. So dominating. This was different, it was personal and intimate. I reached out to brush a lock of dark hair that had fallen across his brow. "And what was that?"

He caught my hand and brought it to his lips, brushing them softly against my knuckles. The tenderness of it transfixed me and I felt my breath catch. But then he released my hand and sighed, wearily. "That some people are just born evil and no amount of wishing or blaming others will change that."

I pulled my hand back and shifted slightly away from him. Simon's confessions were hitting too close to home. He seemed to notice where my thoughts drifted.

"If you allow me to ask another question, lass, I promise two fantasies fulfilled at once."

I snorted with laughter but then noticed he wasn't joking and the sudden images and ideas that filled my mind had my body tightening with desire. But I shook my head. "I don't know that we have time for more questions or fantasies fulfilled. Don't you have to get back to your team soon?"

A look of disappointment seemed to pass over his face, but before he could argue, I continued on. "So I'll accept an IOU instead." I grinned. "Did you really think I'd pass up an opportunity like that?"

He laughed. It was deep, rumbling, and another part of me lit up like a live wire. "Aye, lass, I'd expect no less from you."

I shrugged. "I know a good deal when I see one. So, what's your next question? And don't think you'll be getting out of your bargain. I fully intend to collect on it."

His features stayed soft, but his eyes grew serious. "What did you learn about Sybil?"

I flinched, and my eyes involuntarily flew to the photo of us on my bookshelf. For some reason, I hadn't been able to bring myself to take it down. Even after I'd left my parents' house and learned the truth about our family and its secrets. Somehow the revelations hadn't really surprised me, however, as if the knowledge had been there the whole time and I'd just ignored it. Shoved it down to create this fictional world where my family was perfect and my sister was the star of our story. Or maybe that was the world she'd convinced me to believe in. My eyes turned from the photo to the books that lined my shelves. Maybe that was her fantasy, and I'd just been forced to live in it.

Simon shifting on the sofa made me realize I'd been silent for a while, but he didn't press me. Just watched me in that quiet way that I was becoming thankful for.

I cleared my throat. "Honestly, nothing that I didn't already know. Sybil has always been Sybil. Just that when we hit our teen years, she became fantastic at pretending she wasn't." I stood up and moved towards the shelf, plucking the photo from it, my fingers tracing over the frame. "I thought I'd kept her killing Daisy a secret from my parents like she wanted. But they still found out." I sighed, remembering how hard it had been for my Mother to speak to me when I'd gone home to confront them. She'd wanted to dismiss my questions and my accusations as 'twisting' my memories of the past. When my dad realized that she was reaching the point of hysteria, he'd asked me to step outside and wait for him while he calmed her down. I'd been sitting on the front porch swing watching the neighbors' cows graze behind their fence when he'd come back out with a cup of coffee and sat next to me to tell me the truth.

"They told her that either she stopped tormenting me or they were going to institution- alize her. And I guess she must have realized their threat was serious because after that, she acted like a normal sister. Sort of." I sighed and placed the picture back. "Sybil was never normal, though. We were never normal. I just didn't realize it until now."

Simon stood as well and came to stand behind me, his arms coming around my waist, his chin resting on the top of my head and I relaxed into the muscled warmth of him. But even as I soaked up the contact and the intimacy, I reminded myself that this was just for now. And that it would not, could not, be forever. His voice rumbled in my ear, "So your parents knew Sybil had a mental illness, but did nothing to help her?"

I shook my head. "No, they never said that. In fact, I think they couldn't say it, because it wasn't true. My dad just said that once they confronted her with everything they knew, they'd told her that either it stopped or that they would have her sent away. And once they threatened that, the torture and the attacks stopped. At least the physical ones." I reached out to touch the photo once more, and I wasn't really sure if

I was speaking to him or myself. "It's like you said. Sometimes there's no explanation for why someone does something terrible. It's just who they are. I've seen insanity. I've seen people driven by greed, by desperation, by guilt. I've seen them do terrible things. But I think, in Sybil, I've truly seen evil."

I pushed away from him, needing the distance from the photo and my thoughts. After the talk with my parents, I'd gone over every memory, every interaction, and every word Sybil had ever spoken to me. I didn't know that I'd ever truly be able to accept that my sister was the person she was. But the truth was staring me in the face. Sybil was evil. A monster wrapped up in a pretty package. One that I knew I'd have to face again one day. I glanced down at my coffee table, remembering her text messages from earlier, and frowned.

Simon seemed to notice the direction of my thoughts. "Have you heard from Sybil since you've been back in the States?"

I looked up from my phone to him and then back down, hesitating on whether I should wiggle out of the question by using our bargain or if I should be honest. I decided I liked the openness we'd been sharing and nodded. "Yes, actually, right before you arrived. She texted me a warning." I picked my phone up off the table and opened it, her messages still on display, then handed it to him to read.

I watched his eyes scan through the text, and then he looked back at me. "She texted this tonight?" I should have been alert to the change in his tone and the way his body had tensed, but I was relaxed from the intimacy we'd been sharing, so I nodded. "Yeah, like I said, right before you got here. Wait, what are you doing to my phone?"

But he wasn't listening because suddenly he'd slammed the phone down on the table with such a force that it shook and the phone exploded in several pieces. "You have 3 minutes to pack a bag and get whatever you need to take with you. You're not coming back to this apartment."

He grabbed the pieces of the phone, sorting through them, until he found the sim card and pocketed it in his jeans. I snapped out of my shocked silence. "Um, I think the fuck not. What the hell Simon! I just got that phone!"

But he wasn't listening to me and instead had turned his attention to tearing apart my lamps, turning over pillows and then grabbed a stool from my bar top table to stand on and look into my ceiling fan. He moved in the frantic but thorough way of one who knew exactly where to look for bugs and wiretaps.

"Simon, you have to stop. I've already looked this place over from one end to the other. You don't think I didn't do that as soon as I got back? I already took care of it." And then I walked over to a little side table and opened up a drawer, showing him the small microphones and wires I'd found planted throughout my apartment upon my return from Helsinki.

He stopped, looked at the drawer and then back at me, but none of the tension left him. "It doesn't matter. You need to get your bags packed now. I'm not giving you another warning. We're leaving."

I slammed the drawer shut and stalked toward him until I was inches from him once more. "What. The. Fuck." My finger jabbed his chest with each word, but he didn't flinch. Just continued to glare at me as if by his gaze alone he could force me to do his will. "I'm not going anywhere, Simon. So you can take this macho over protective bullshit you've got going on and just fuck right off with it." We glared at each other for a few heartbeats. Our faces so close that our breath mingled, and I tried not to get distracted by the fullness of his lips or the way his body heat made mine react. Finally he spoke, his jaw clenched so tight I thought I could hear his bones grinding. "I can't protect you here, Hannah. I can't keep you safe from her." I blinked in startlement.

"I don't need your protection. I know who my sister is." I softened my voice just slightly, but still held his gaze. "I'm not Victoria."

He flinched, stepping back slightly as if by speaking her name I'd put a barrier between us, and searched my gaze in that intense way that left me feeling open and exposed. Go ahead and analyze every inch of me, buddy. I'm not Tory. I've got nothing to hide. And I'm not afraid. After a moment more, he nodded. "You're right. You aren't Victoria." He paused again, his jaw clenching and unclenching as if he was searching for the words to say. "I have to go."

CHAPTER SEVEN

Hannah

It felt like the walls we'd torn down over the evening were being slammed back into place. "Go? What do you mean?"

Someone knocked loudly on my apartment door, but I was the only one who jumped at the sudden sound. My eyes flicked from the door to Simon, whose face was once again an unreadable mask. Gone was the intimacy from earlier. Gone was the softness and the tenderness. Simon the Ghost was back. The knock came again, and I looked at the door. "Expecting someone?"

He said nothing and so I went to open it once again, blinking in surprise. "Colonel Abrams, what are you doing here?"

The tall man was no longer in his military

uniform, but rather a dark blue button-down shirt that stretched across a broad chest, sculpted shoulders, and made his sapphire colored eyes gleam in the hall's dim lighting. The only thing that would have clued anyone into the fact that he was a military man was the cut of his hair and the way he carried himself. He was commanding, even standing in my doorway. He gave me a charming smile, his gaze flicking over my shoulder to Simon, who was standing like a dark shadow at my back. "I'm his...." But he was cut off as Simon interrupted him.

"He's my ride. Can you give me a minute, Jon? I'll be right down."

Jon's eyes narrowed for a split second, his easy going grin suddenly becoming too easy, too bright, too hard. It was as if he was sending a silent message to Simon that was more a threat than an acquiesce. "Fine, but I'll be just outside the door."

I frowned at the exchange between the two men and shut my door as Jon turned to move down the hall and wait.

"What was that about? Is he your handler now?"

Simon's face was hardened marble as he pressed against me until my back was flush with the door, his hand gripping my jaw and tilting my chin up. He bent down and the kiss he gave me held none of the tenderness or longing from earlier. It was hard and demanding. His lips and tongue coaxing over mine as if he was trying to search out every part of my soul, every drop of my being and pour back into me with everything that he was.

I held back at first, anger, confusion and the demand for answers warring within me. But then I was kissing him back. Our mouths clashed, and I heard a low rumble in his chest as he groaned when one of my legs raised to hook around his waist, drawing him in closer. I couldn't, wouldn't, resist him. Then, just as suddenly as it began, it stopped, and he drew away from me, his breathing heavy and eyes dark with desire and other emotions I didn't understand yet.

"I can't explain what's going on. But I have to go." His words were heavy with unspoken feelings and my heart winced at the pleading in them. "Please Hannah, I know I don't deserve this from you, but please lass, if you need help, get word to Michael or Rue. They'll know what to do."

Tiny fractures of pain flared in my heart. Pain that I quickly squashed with anger as my eyes slitted and my lips curled into a snarl. "You had no intention of keeping your promise, did you?"

He said nothing, but I saw something dark flicker in the gun metal colored depths of his eyes.

"Tell me you didn't come here and feed me

another lie, Simon Gallagher. Tell me you didn't come here just to get information out of me. Tell me you didn't use me again."

His silence thundered louder than any confession he could have made, and those tiny fractures shattered into a thousand pieces. Red crept into my gaze as I moved away from the door, but my voice was cold and flat as I spoke.

"Well, Mr. Gallagher, I have to give you credit. Your acting is impeccable. Academy Award-winning acting classes must be standard with international asshole spy training." I moved to the side and gripped the door handle. "Tell Michael, Rue and Evan I said that I'm genuinely sorry for everything they had to go through because of me and my sister. But I think it's time we officially ended our professional relationship." I opened the door. "Goodbye Mr. Gallagher."

"Hannah..." His voice was a low groan, a plea, but I cut him off by opening the door wider and stepping out into the hall, where Colonel Abrams took notice and moved towards us.

"He's all yours Colonel."

Simon didn't glance at the officer, just gave me one last long look before striding past me toward the elevator doors at the end of my hall. I didn't turn around to see if he looked back. I was sure he wouldn't.

Jon watched him walk away for a second and then looked down at me and I steeled myself for whatever question he had forming on the tip of his tongue but then something he saw in my gaze made him think twice and he just shook his head, moving in closer to where I was standing still holding my door open. I had to tip my head back to continue to look at him properly, his height topping Simon's by at least two or three inches, and I briefly wondered if he was aware of how much of a target that would make him.

"Ms. Kelly, I wonder, does the FBI know what kind of talent they're letting go to waste under their roof?"

I blinked, unsure of if I'd heard him correctly. "I'm sorry. What did you say?"

"Well," He nodded his head down the hall at Simon's retreating back. "I just witnessed one of the most formidable espionage agents in the business run out of your apartment scared shitless without a shot fired, an explosion, or a threat of nuclear war hanging in the balance." He gave me half a grin. "If that's not talent, I'm not sure what is."

I smirked, allowing myself a small smile at his

attempt at a joke, and shook my head. "Sorry, but the only person Simon Gallagher fears is a ghost. And I'm not referring to his job description."

The colonel's eyes glinted with sympathy. "You're right. Simon is haunted by far more than the sins of his past. But I wasn't kidding about wasted talent." He held something out to me and I found myself taking a crisp white business card from him. A business card that looked eerily similar to one Simon had left a note on my door with so many weeks ago. I frowned, looking at the blank card, and held it up between my fingers. "A blank business card? I didn't know the Department of Defense was in the business of playing magic tricks, Colonel."

"Look closer, Ms. Kelly. Everything you need to know is on that business card. As you can probably guess, my role at the Pentagon is more fluid than a uniform would let you believe." He cocked his head, a smirk playing about his full lips as I continued to study the card. I frowned as something reflected in the light and as I twisted and turned its edges, I saw the silver outline of a symbol etched into the grain of the cardstock. It was a small cube hidden within a second larger cube, outlined by a ring. An enigma symbol. I looked up at the towering man, who was watching me with intense interest.

"What exactly are you asking me, Colonel?"

"Officially?" His grin widened, a tactic that was probably meant to be disarming but only made me think of a predator showing off his razor-sharp teeth. "Nothing. I am just here to escort Mr. Gallagher to where he needs to go." He leaned down and tapped the business card I still held out in front me. I could smell the subtle scent of his aftershave and stiffened with the urge to back away, but didn't. "But unofficially? People have heard about your exploits and you've gained some attention in other circles. They think you'd be a great asset and if you're ever tired of playing patty-cake with the bureau, you may just have other avenues of employment to explore."

I looked at the card; the symbol glinting like a silvery beacon now that I knew where to look, then to the handsome man whose gaze never wavered, but whose smile didn't quite reach his eyes. "They think I'd be a great asset? Or you..." my words trailed off as I gauged his reaction, but those dark blue eyes gave away nothing. "Tell me, Ms. Kelly, do you really think the Abromov group and the Hildago Syndicate will ever truly disappear? Do you think organizations like that just fade away?" He shook his head. "No, they're just spiders linked in one giant web. The minute one spider is exterminated, another rises to take its place." He just turned around, long legs carrying him toward the elevators, calling back to me.

"Just think about it, Ms. Kelly. If you're interested, I'm sure you'll figure out a way to contact me."

I didn't bother to respond or ask him how he knew that I'd find a way to reach him. I just watched the symbol appear and disappear as I held the card under the light. Shiny, silvery, almost translucent. Like a ghost.

Yeah, I knew exactly how to contact him. The question was, did I want to?

CHAPTER EIGHT

Hannah

My eyes flew open to darkness. That was nothing new. I wasn't able to sleep unless it was completely dark, shades drawn, not a single light on in the room. Years of night shift duties had made it so that I needed total darkness and blackout curtains to sleep, even if it wasn't during the day. I laid in bed, my breaths coming slow and steady as my senses took in the inky blackness of my room. The darkness was nothing new, but the presence I felt was.

Every nerve tingled on high alert. The soft tick of my old-fashioned alarm clock was the only sound penetrating the dark. Carefully, subtle inch by subtle inch, I slid my hand from where I'd fallen asleep cradling my head, to underneath my pillow.

My movements were slow, timed with the rise and fall of my breathing. I felt my burner phone first, the only phone I had since Simon had destroyed my other one, and praying it was still on silent, I hit just one button before reaching further. When my fingers felt the cool hardness of my suppressed weapon, I paused, waiting.

Then I heard it. The whisper of movement was so soft and subtle that if I hadn't been on alert, or still asleep, I would have missed it. The weight of a step as it slid towards my bed. I tensed. My breath held. And then the darkness exploded.

A large hand landed a heavy blow to my head as I tried to sit up, whipping my gun from under the pillow to fire off a single shot. I was rewarded with a grunt, even as my ears were ringing and pain bloomed on the side of my head. They'd grazed me, whoever it was, but the blow had definitely been meant to knock me out, or worse. I heard a muffled curse and my bedroom door banged open, nearly coming off its hinges, as a second person barged through. The darkness of my apartment did little to allow more light in, but it was just enough that I could make out hulking shadows as I rolled to the far side of my bed and slid to the floor.

"Where is she?" The voice was rough and heavily accented. A low groan of pain answered in return. They couldn't see me, but weren't turning on the lights. I wondered what that meant but then didn't have time to think about it anymore as I heard the distinct slide of a safety being let off and then the room was encased in orange and reds as bullets sprayed where my body had been on the bed. I scooted towards the far side of my room as debris and casings rained down. Then I realized why they weren't turning on the lights. They were stupid. Because if they'd been smart, they would have blinded me during the brief adjustment time my eyes would need to go from darkness to blinding light, and could have easily overtaken me. As it was, goon number one was slumped back against my closet door, his stricken figure illuminated in the blaze of light coming from the muzzle fire that goon number two was destroying my mattress with. Something about their stupidity and the sight of my bed getting turned inside out pissed me off and without thinking I fired off two more shots, but they went wide grazing goon two's shoulder and lodging in the plaster next to his head.

"Fuck." I didn't have time to think or be pissed anymore. Goon two had recovered and now knew where my exact position was. He swung the barrel of his semi-auto around, bullets spraying in an arc that shattered my mirror and the few picture frames I'd had on the walls behind me. I launched myself forward, instinct driving me, and tackled his legs. My arms wrapped around his knees and he was knocked down with a solid thunk to the ground. He wasn't a big man, but I knew I'd never win the fight for his gun and it was too close quarters to make the attempt so I did the next best thing and in my scramble to get to my feet dropped my knee straight down into his junk.

I was rewarded with a howl of pain and string of curses but didn't bother checking on the damage I'd left behind, just continued my scramble forward until I'd climbed over him and reached my bedroom door. Then I was in my short hallway and racing towards my front door. I was stopped short when my nose hit a brick wall. Only it wasn't a wall, it was a chest. A very muscular chest. Driven by instinct and training once more, I dropped my shoulder, reaching for the man's arm and drove my hip into his even as I was turning my body and using the off balance weight of him to flip him to the floor.

"Ooof, Hannah! Stop!" The gruff voice snapped at me and I dropped the arm I was attempting to twist out of its socket.

"Michael?" I hissed in surprise but then didn't

have time to ask anymore questions. "Come on bro, we need to get out of here."

Michael stood just as we heard movement from my back bedroom. Goon two had apparently caught his breath enough to come after me and was scrambling towards the hallway. Michael snapped at me again, "Go, Hannah. Rue is waiting. I'll take care of this."

"What?" I blinked and then once more was diving towards cover behind my couch as gunfire erupted around us. Michael landed only half a second behind me and I saw the glint of his weapon just seconds before he flipped around and returned fire.

Suddenly, the gunfire stopped and a lull of silence enveloped us with only the sound of our heavy breathing and heartbeats pounding in our ears.

"Is he..." I let my whisper trail off and Michael said nothing, just motioned for me to stay put where I'd wedged myself between the couch and my bookshelves, before slinking off into the darkness. I glanced from Michael's retreating figure to the front door, calculating how long it would take me to leap the couch and make my escape should bullets start flying again.

But then I didn't have to worry about it as

Michael returned holding a bloody semi-automatic rifle in his hands. Dark eyes glinted in the whisper of moonlight that filtered through my living room windows, and I took a quick glance at the destruction around me. My books. My floor was littered with the fluttering pages of destroyed books. I didn't ask what had happened to the two men in my bedroom. If Michael hadn't finished them, I was going to.

I looked back at Michael, who had moved to the window and was peering through my blinds at something below. "You got here fast."

He grunted, "Something told me I needed to be close by."

I cocked my head. "Something? Or someone?"

He slid a glance to me, a dark eyebrow cocked upward. "Does it really matter?"

I sighed and shook my head, once more taking in the chaotic destruction of my apartment. "No, I guess it doesn't. Not anymore." I waved a hand at the mess. "I don't suppose you can fairy godmother this shit and make it all go away?" I wasn't just referring to the blood and mess and something in my face must have given away my thoughts because for a moment Michael's eyes softened and he pulled out his phone. "I'll see what I can do. But we need to go. The police will be on their way. You have everything?" When I nodded, he motioned with the weapon he was still holding to the hallway and bedrooms. "Is this Sybil's handiwork?"

I shook my head. "I'm not one hundred percent sure, but I don't think it was Sybil. I think they were goons sent by the Hildago Syndicate." Michael frowned, a concerned look passing over his face and I asked. "You know them?"

He nodded, "Yes. My family has had dealings with them in the past. They're a nasty bunch. How did you get caught up with them?"

I sighed. "It's a long story. I'll catch you up."

Grabbing my bag I'd stashed in my coat closet, a jacket and slipped into a pair of Converse before I headed to the door but paused with my hand on the handle as something sticking out of the pile of papers on my entryway table caught my eye. A blank white business card.

Without thinking, I snatched it up and shoved it into a side pocket. Pigs would fly before I'd ever go back to the FBI after everything I'd seen and been through. But I'd be damned if I was going to let my sister, or anyone else, dictate my life choices anymore. Simon might not want me in his little secret spy club, but there was no way he could keep me out, either. I smirked, wondering what Simon would have said about tonight, and headed towards the elevators, leaving my bloody mess of an apart-ment behind just as I heard the sound of approaching sirens. I didn't worry about Michael getting out of there, knowing that he was just as capable as Simon of getting out of squirrelly situa-tions. How he planned to make the mess look less like a shoot house and more like a....I didn't even know what. I couldn't imagine what the cops, some who were probably my friends, would say when they saw the place. But those were problems for tomorrow Hannah. Tonight Hannah had bigger things to worry about. Like the fact that a murderous crime syndicate might have sent someone to assassinate her. And that her psychotic and sadistic sister, who was hell bent on killing her, had tried to warn her. "What kind of game are you playing, Sybil? "I muttered to myself as I opened the emergency exit door and descended the steps to the parking garage below.

It might have been my imagination and the stress of the night, but a silky voice whispered through the darkness of my thoughts. "You'll see..."

CHAPTER NINE

Hannah

When I'd gotten into Michael's waiting Lexus SUV, and I knew it was his by the blacked out and heavily tinted everything, Rue was waiting for me with a cup of coffee and a smile. I blinked in shock but took the cup from her, frowning at the lid and then back up at the beautiful hacker who was watching me.

"Thank you, but please forgive me if I ask you if this is poisoned or not." Rue's smile only widened, which had me lowering the cup to place it in a cup holder until I could verify its contents.

Rue tsked, "Cheri, unlike my stubborn male counterparts, I don't want to hold grudges." Her eyes hardened. "What you did was cold, calculated and an absolute betrayal of our trust." They softened just a bit. "But I understand why you did it. And I might have made the same choice."

I picked up the coffee, taking a sip and leaned back in my seat. "Forgive me Rue, I didn't mean to make you upset."

"You should really learn to test for poisons before you so easily trust the word of an assassin."

I choked on the hot liquid, sputtering. "What?!"

She flashed a grin. "Kidding!! Oh, but here." She whipped out a napkin and handed it to me. "Better wipe that up before Michael gets back. He had a fit that I made him stop for coffee on the way here. The psychopath doesn't allow anyone to eat or drink in his precious vehicles.'

I took the offered napkin and began dabbing away at any droplets that may have clung to the leather upholstery. "You mean to tell me that while I was fighting for my life, you two were out making a coffee run?" I asked incredulously. "So glad I was alive to drink it!"

She cocked her head, wide eyes blinking at me. "Hannah, part of being on a team is trusting that one of your team members can handle themselves in any situation." She reached across the seat and laid a hand on my knee. "Tell me, when Michael got to you, did you need him?"

I stared at her for a moment, dumbstruck by

her words. They trusted me to handle myself without back-up, but they would never have left me to flounder on my own. "No, I didn't. I'd killed the first guy and wounded the second. I could have taken him out myself, but then Michael was there." Realization struck, Michael hadn't been there to save me. He'd been there to help me clean up.

She offered a soft smile and squeezed my knee. "And that is why we stopped for coffee. You don't need us, Hannah. You never did."

I didn't have much time to think about her words before Michael was back and sliding into the driver's seat. Then we were speeding off through the night, just as the blue and red lights of Atlanta's finest began bouncing off the concrete walls of the surrounding buildings.

Michael's black gaze found mine in the rearview mirror. "You know he's going to find out."

I huffed and looked out my window at the buildings that were passing by in a blur. "Let him. Simon doesn't control what I do."

Michael's dark chuckle filtered through the SUV. "Hannah, trust me, the last thing Simon wants to do is control you." My gaze flicked back to find his in the rear view mirror and saw a concerned look there. "He's just worried about you."

The last person I wanted to discuss at the

moment was Simon and his motivations for anything that concerned me, so I switched the topics and held up the white business card. "Anyone care to tell me what this is all about?"

Rue and Michael shared a glance between them as if they were carrying on a silent conversation. When Rue raised one eyebrow and Michael turned back to glare silently at the road ahead, I knew who had won the argument.

She turned her golden gaze to me. "That, ma chéri, is the calling card of the Enigma Group and technically, our employer."

It was my turn to arch an eyebrow. "And why does Colonel Abrams think that I'd be a good recruit for your 'employer'?

Rue shrugged and gave me a conspiratorial smile, "Probably because you've been running circles around these Neanderthals he's in charge of and wants to see what kind of havoc you can create if he unleashes you onto the criminal underworld?"

I snorted and flipped the card in my fingers. "Havoc seems to be what I'm good at. I don't know if it's super secret spy worthy though."

Rue shrugged, "Well, someone thinks you're good enough to be considered as a candidate. The Enigma Group isn't just a spy agency. It's the premier spy organization in the world. In order to be asked to join, you have to be vetted and then referred by someone very high up in the chain of command. And then you're thoroughly investigated and tested in order to even get the invite." She reached over and tapped the card. That you have that card means you've passed several of their gates already and they are very interested in getting you into their fold."

I studied the card in my hand. "But I don't get it. Who would refer me? Did one of you?"

She shook her head. "Sorry, chéri. I'm not high enough to hand off a referral like that." When I cast a questioning look at Michael, he shook his head as well. "Don't look at me, doll. I think you've got the balls, yeah, but I'm still on probation with the Enigma group command team. They aren't happy that I'm still connected to my familia."

I frowned and tucked the card back into my pocket. It didn't make sense, but I didn't have the bandwidth to reason through the why's or how at the moment. Instead, I pulled out the burner phone and handed it to Michael. "Here, thank you for this. You were right, and they completely tapped my house, including my phone."

Michael just grunted. "Keep it. It came in handy tonight."

I shook my head. "Michael I can't. I'm being

hunted by two different crime organizations now. I appreciate you guys coming to the rescue tonight, but I need to lie low for a while and can't risk anyone being able to trace me." I glanced from Rue to Michael, who were once again sharing a silent conversation between them and realization dawned. "Hey, weren't you guys supposed to be on your way to meet Simon, anyway? I thought you were both long gone by now."

A guilty look flashed across Rue's features and she turned around to face me. "I'm sorry, Hannah. Please don't be upset. It's not that we didn't trust you but, in our line of work, there's always a contingency plan."

I blinked. "You mean a contingency plan in case I wasn't able to get Simon out of federal prison?"

Rue shook her head. "No mon ami, a contingency plan in case Agent Reed caught word of what you'd planned to do and they arrested you as well."

I frowned, my thoughts a whirling tornado in my head, and looked at the phone, then back to Michael and Rue. "I don't know that I'll ever understand or be comfortable with the layers of deception and lies you guys seem to swim in." I tucked the phone back into my jacket pocket. "But for once, I'm thankful for it."

Rue offered me a gentle smile. "So, what is the plan now?"

I sighed and settled back in my seat as we raced towards the team's penthouse. "Now? I need to find out who put the hit out on me."

Michael spoke up. "Do you want any help with that?"

I glanced at him, feeling more than grateful for the ex-special forces soldier and wayward mafia prince. More than once since we'd left Helsinki, Michael had been there to help me. His family's connections to Interpol had gotten him out of custody sooner than anyone else and he'd contacted me before I'd even gotten back to the states. I'd thought that out of all of them, other than Simon, Michael would be the most furious with me. He was the one who'd trusted me the least. But all he'd said was, "Get Simon out of prison and take care of Rue. Then your debt to me is paid." Since then, he'd supplied me with the burner phone and the information I'd needed to get into contact with Simon's handlers. "If it will not put you in any more debt with your familia, then yes, that would be great. I wore my connections at the bureau out. I don't think I can count on anyone to help me out at the moment."

Rue's lips twisted upward in a sinister grin.

"Well, well, look at you, miss Federal Agent. Are you saying you're ready to play a little dirty?"

I snickered, but the laugh sounded hollow to my own ears and I continued to watch the buildings blur by us. "Rue, honey, you have no idea how dirty I can play."

CHAPTER TEN

Hannah

Red clay stained the soles of my white tennis shoes, making it look like I'd just walked through a puddle of rust instead of the little garden path that led to my Memaw's back porch. Raised garden beds filled with green plants and freshly grown vegetables lined either side of the little walkway. I could hear the squeak of her rocking chair as I approached the porch.

"Hannah Marie, you better get on up here and tell me what's the matter with you. I could hear you hollerin' all the way down the road."

I sniffed, rubbing my tear-stained face with the back of my hand. How the old woman knew I'd been crying was a mystery. I hadn't even made a sound as I'd raced from our house and around the pond that was in the back of our property to the little gate that separated our place from Memaw's.

"I wasn't cryin', Memaw." I pouted stubbornly as I approached the patio. She sat in her old rocking chair, a large white bowl placed next to her on a small wooden table and at her feet was a sack filled to the brim with freshly picked green beans. She'd grab a handful, snap the ends off with nimble fingers and fling them in the bowl. Rock, reach, snap, snap, drop. Over and over again until the bowl was full, or she'd run out of beans.

"Don't sass me, girl. You don't think I didn't watch you run all the way over here like your tail was on fire? I thought you were supposed to be having a sleepover with friends today."

I climbed the steps and dropped onto a low stool next to her. She didn't pause in her rhythm, just scooted the sack of beans closer to me and gave me a nudge with her shoe. "Go on, get you a handful and tell me about it. What did your sister do this time?"

"Nothing." I grabbed a handful of beans and settled into the rhythmic ritual that had become our almost daily habit. When the world felt off, I could almost always count on my Memaw to set it right.

"Hannah, God don't like liars. Tell me what happened."

"That's just it Memaw. Nothing happened. Sybil didn't do anything this time."

My grandmother paused her rocking. "Well, what in the world has got your britches in a twist? And don't tell me nothin', cuz somethin' happened or you wouldn't be here bothering me." She huffed and the rock, reach, snap, snap continued on.

"It's my friends Memaw.. They don't even know I exist when Sybil is around."

"So tell your sister to get lost." The gruff and direct voice made me almost smile. Memaw was no nonsense in a way that I wished I could be. Maybe that's why I'd come to her to begin with.

"I can't Memaw. Sybil doesn't actually do anything. She's just there. But when she's there, I'm not." I looked down at the beans I'd been snapping and sighed.

My Memaw said nothing for a moment, but when she did speak her voice was quiet but firm. "Hannah Marie Kelly, you are not invisible and no one can make you feel that way unless you give them that power." She reached down and grabbed my chin in her gnarled hands and I breathed in the familiar scent of lotion and earth. "When you decide to stop giving her the power to dictate who you are, then you'll discover just how bright you can shine. You are light, Hannah, and the dark has always been afraid of the light. It's why it tries to cover it up."

. . .

For the second time in twenty-four hours, I woke to someone in my room. Only this time, the darkness didn't feel like danger, and the room wasn't really mine. Michael and Rue had brought me back to the team penthouse for the night and I'd only agreed to stay after they'd insisted it was the safest place for me to be for the time being. After showering and removing the blood and scent of gunpowder from my body, I'd collapsed on the guest room bed in exhaustion. But sleep hadn't come easily and after tossing and turning, I'd finally drifted off.

My heart hurt at the memory of my Memaw. It wasn't just a dream I'd had. Something about her words and the memory from my childhood stayed with me. Was Sybil really afraid of me? What was it about me that had made her hate me so much? What did I represent that she couldn't have? I blinked in the dim, early morning sunlight that was filtering through my drapes and sighed.

"If you came to tell me 'I told you so.' You'd better have brought coffee and a donut to go along with it."

A deep chuckle filled the room, and I watched as his tall figure emerged from the shadows, with a coffee in one hand and a donut in the other. "It's not an 'I told you so.' But more of a peace offering."

I sat up; the covers falling from my shoulders, and scooted back against my pillows as he approached.

"I thought you were off on a quest for Abrams?" I took the coffee and donut from him as he slid onto the bed next to me.

"I told Abrams to call off his hounds for a little while longer. This was more important." Dark grey eyes glinted in the low light, and a soft smile turned at the corner of his lips. "I don't like things left unfinished or unsaid."

The coffee was hot and rich dark mocha and I nearly groaned out loud in satisfaction, but paused at his words. "What do you mean?"

"I mean, I left you without finishing what I'd promised." His smile sharpened, white teeth glinting like a predator, and I snorted.

"Si, stop. It was a stupid, silly game we shouldn't have played. It's ok if you didn't mean it."

He leaned in, dark eyes serious as an intensity settled over him. "No, Hannah, we're not doing this. I'm tired of playing word games with you, lass. When I saw Sybil's messages to you, I panicked. It felt like Tory all over again, with Sybil playing her games. All I could see was the danger you are in."

He paused, one of his hands reaching for mine as he drew it to his lips. "I wanted you the moment

I met you. I wanted you more the moment you opened your mouth and told me to fuck right off." His lips trailed a line from the palm of my hand to my wrist and my flesh pebbled where he hovered over my pulse.

"I was a broken man when I met you, Hannah Kelly. I was never more scared than when I realized the danger I'd put you in. But then you handled it brilliantly. You took everything I and your sister threw at you and you gave it right back to us. You handed me my ass and stole my heart at the same time."

My breath caught as his words resonated inside of me. I watched as he turned my palm over and then drew me forward until he'd placed it flat against his chest, his heartbeat thundering beneath it. "Do you feel that, Hannah? That was dead before you."

"Simon I..." He cut me off.

"You don't owe me anything. I overreacted last night because I couldn't handle the idea that your sister could get to you like that. But I should know by now that if anyone can handle Sybil, it would be you. I swear I wasn't there for any other reason than that I wanted to be. I wasn't trying to use you Hannah, I'd just wanted to see you one more time, and I was using any excuse I could think of to give me a reason to be there." He shook his head and gave a soft, chuffing laugh. "For once, there wasn't a reason for me to lie or scheme or manipulate anything. But I did it anyway because I was afraid that if I showed up and was just honest about how I felt, you'd slam the door in my face."

I swallowed past the lump in my throat, my heart pounding in my ears as his words as their meaning registered. "And how do you feel?" The words were whispered, and I wasn't even sure I'd said them out loud.

His eyes darkened as he watched my teeth nervously nibble at the bottom of my lip. Dropping my hand, he leaned in closer, his hand coming to cup the side of my face, thumb tracing my lip. "Like without you, I can't breathe. Like everything in my life led to the moment that I first saw you in that interrogation room. Like before then, I was just a dead man walking and the only thing I had to live for was some sorry excuse for revenge. Like I would go through everything, Victoria, Sybil, the Abromov group, just to walk into that interrogation room again."

My breath caught and once again I was struck dumb by his words. His thumb continued his exploration of my lip and his eyes searched mine in that quiet way that told me he knew what I was thinking before I'd even had a chance to express it. "Don't say anything, Hannah. I didn't come here to convince you to come with me, or to persuade you to do anything. I just needed you to know that you did that to me. You set me free."

I exhaled and said the only thing that felt right and true in a long time. "I love you too, Simon Gallagher."

CHAPTER ELEVEN

Simon

My heart stuttered.

Whatever I'd been expecting by coming here to confess how I felt, it hadn't been that. But it was as if she'd woken up, and like the sleep from her eyes, had dropped the walls guarding her heart. I didn't realize we'd moved toward each other until her hands were pulling at my shirt and her mouth was moving over mine. I groaned, the need for her filling me until I thought I was going to burst if I couldn't get inside her right then.

The covers were pulled completely away, and I was greeted with the view of her in nothing but an oversized t-shirt and lace panties. Pushing her back on the bed, she responded with a husky moan as my hand palmed her pussy and I felt the wetness there.

I pulled her panties to the side, fingers gently tracing between the wet folds. She pulled her mouth away from mine and panted, desperate. "Si..."

I grinned, pulling the t-shirt up until her breasts were exposed and I could pull one dusky nipple into my mouth. She arched against me and I sucked harder, tongue swirling the sensitive tip.

"Tell me what you want, Hannah."

She growled, "Simon..." I bit down on her nipple and withdrew my fingers to just the edge of her opening.

"I told you Hannah. I want to fulfill every filthy fantasy you have. Tell what you want, lass."

Her eyes flew open, and she looked down at me where I'd pulled back and switched to her other breast, giving it the same attention.

"You, Simon. I want all of you. Don't hold back."

I stilled and looked up at her. Her green eyes were bright with desire and sincerity. "You're sure, love?"

Her only response was to arch against me again, rubbing her slickness against my hand, and moan. "Please, Simon..."

I was undone. Her hands flicked at the zipper of my pants and in one smooth motion, I drew them down and tossed them onto the floor next to us. In the next instance, I'd ripped away the thin scrap of fabric that covered her entrance and lined my cock up, pausing for just a brief second to look down and marvel at the sight of her.

"Look, Hannah, look at what you do to me, lass." She licked her lips and rocked her hips once more, her wetness coating my cock.

"Feel that, Simon? Feel how wet I am? That's what *you* do to me."

I surged forward, burying myself in her heat. The rhythm that took over had me driving into her again and again. The little noises she made and the throaty way she cried out as her release took her nearly made me come apart inside of her right then.

I pulled out to a whimper of disappointment, but quickly flipped her over and drew her to her knees. "Shhh, lass, you said you wanted me. So take it." I gripped her hair, drawing her head back. "Show me you can take it." I growled. And then I surged into her again, driving forward with punishing strokes, my cock gliding over every sensi-tive part of her and not stopping until I'd filled her as deep as I could go. And then I drew out nearly to the tip before slamming home again.

Her breasts bounced the force of my thrusts. Her throat and head tilted back as a low moan escaped her parted lips as her orgasm built. Reaching beneath her, I felt the wetness that dripped down her thighs and found her sweet center there. A few circled flicks with my thumb and she was screaming, her release gushing around me as she collapsed forward.

My thrusts faltered, my release building, and then seconds later, I was collapsing with her. We didn't speak, just laid there together, still joined, and I nearly became hard again thinking about being inside of her still. When her breathing came back to normal, I drew her back against me, nuzzling the back of her neck and breathing in the scent of vanilla and jasmine.

I couldn't stop touching her. My hands wandered from her throat to the fullness of her breast, lifting and cupping them in my hands before letting them drop again and continuing my explorations. Her stomach was flat but still soft, her hips full and rounded. I could have spent hours tracing the softness of her skin.

She moaned and tilted her head back, allowing me more access to the sensitive side of her neck.

"Keep that up, Mr. Gallagher, and you might have to make good on your two for one deal."

I grinned, nipping at the spot between her neck

and collarbone. "Still sounds like I get the better end of the bargain, love."

"Mmmm..." She wiggled against me and I groaned in response as I felt the blood rushing to my dick again.

"Aye, lass, don't tempt me unless you're ready for it." I growled against her neck, my hand slipping down to tease the slickness between her thighs. Something about the idea that her come and mine mingled there had me suddenly raging hard, and I prayed that she was ready for me again, because I didn't know if I had the self-control to stop at this point.

She laughed, a full and throaty sound that had my heart doing somersaults. "Simon, there's nothing you could give me I can't handle. I'm always ready for it." She paused and I could hear a sudden hesitation in her voice.

"But?" I pushed, even as I teased apart her folds and traced a slow circle around her sensitive nub.

"Buuuuut...." She drew the word out in a moan and licked her lips, her hips mimicking the circle of my fingers against my hand. "Jesus, Simon, I can't think when you do that."

"Good." I pinched her nipple with my free hand and added more pressure to her clit with my other. "I only want you thinking about this right now."

I knew where her mind had wandered to. What about after? What about when early morning turned into day and the sunshine brought all the problems and things that got in the way with it? I didn't have an answer for her yet. Not a good one, at least. All I could do was give her what I could in the now and hold on to that for whatever happened in the future.

I rolled onto my back, taking her with me, and she turned until she was straddling me, my thickness sliding through her folds. Her eyes were half closed, and she purred as she rubbed herself against me, teasing the opening but not sliding her heat down onto me.

"Are you trying to distract me?" She grinned, and I gripped her hips, dragging her hard against my cock.

"Aye, is it working?"

She sat forward slightly, her breasts swaying just out of reach of my mouth, and I groaned. What had I been thinking? She was going to be the death of me. "Aye," she mimicked my accent, and I grinned. And then she was sliding her wet heat down the length of my head, tipping back as a low throaty moan escaped her lips.

She took her time, her body finding an unhurried rhythm as she rose above me. The feel of her gripping me, her hips swirling in a sensual circle, the way she closed her eyes and arched back as she completely gave herself over to seeking her release, drove me wild. It was all I could do to not flip her over again and claim her the way I wanted to. Because I knew without a doubt that this woman was mine and I was hers.

I drove my hips upwards suddenly as possessiveness overcame me and her eyes fluttered open. But she just shot me a cocky smirk and met me thrust for thrust, losing herself into the pounding pace I set.

The morning and everything else that came with it be damned. Nothing and no-one was taking this woman away from me again.

"I love you, Hannah." I sat up suddenly, pulling her to me and capturing her mouth in a punishing kiss as I continued rocking into her. Her body quaked around me as she moaned. "Yes, Simon. I'm yours."

CHAPTER TWELVE

Hannah

I splashed cold water on my face and straight-ened to look at the woman in the mirror. Simon had stayed with me until a message from Abrams had pulled him reluctantly from the bed. We'd spent the morning talking about anything and everything but the situation at hand. He'd told me stories from his time in the military and all the trouble Evan had gotten him into. I told him about my days growing up in the country and my Memaw. We'd laughed, made love, and finally, when he couldn't stay a second longer, he'd left after giving me a heated kiss with two words. "Be careful."

I stared at my reflection and sighed. How the fuck was I supposed to be careful with not one, but possibly two, angry criminal organizations after me?

Not to mention the unfinished business with my psychotic sister. What was her game? Why had she sent me that warning? I almost reached for my phone to review the messages, but then remembered Simon had destroyed it.

"And took the damn sim card. Son of a bitch!" I slammed my palm down on the counter in annoyance at not remembering that detail while he was here. If I could have gotten the sim card back, I might have been able to pull the data from it to find out where Sybil had been texting me from. Whirling away from the sink, I stalked towards the bedroom door, determined to find Michael or Rue and track down Simon.

When I got to the penthouse living room, I was greeted with a sweeping view of the downtown area of Buckhead, a suburb of Atlanta, and the main financial district of the city. The wealth here came mostly from bankers, hedge fund managers and big movers in the financial world. However, more recently, it had drawn the attention of Atlanta's thriving music and entertainment business. Rappers, singers, actors, and producers all enjoyed the access to wealth and luxury shopping from the famed Lenox mall. It wasn't uncommon to see Bugatti's, Ferrari's and other cars so expensive, I doubted I would ever be able to pronounce their name, drive down the street and make a C-class Mercedes look average.

The main sitting area was a sunken living room boasting white leather couches that faced a modern fireplace and a giant screen TV. When I'd stayed here the first time, the team had told me they only kept the place for appearances when they needed to meet with important or influential sources. Otherwise, they preferred to maintain their own residences and conducted their operations from different safe houses around the world. It made sense to have Atlanta as a base like this, considering its airport was one of the biggest international hubs of transportation.

Across from the living room was an open kitchen with modern cabinetry and state-of-the-art appliances. Lining the outer wall between the two spaces was a seamless line of windows that you could view nearly all the city from. During the day, electronic shutters kept most of the glare from the sun out, but at night, I'd witnessed the city lights sparkling and dancing before me brighter than the stars in the sky.

Michael was leaning against the kitchen island staring down at his phone with his ever present scowl. Rue was sitting at the breakfast table, the laptop she seemed to never be far from open, her fingers flying over the keys as she bobbed her head to whatever music was bumping through her turquoise, soundproof headphones.

"Morning." I mumbled as I approached the island where Michael was standing. He looked up and gave me a curt nod before glancing back down at his phone. I frowned at the rudeness and flipped him the bird as I was rounding the counters, heading towards the coffee pot. I didn't think he'd seen my gesture, but then I let out a huff of laughter as his finger shot up and he returned it without even breaking contact with the phone screen.

I was pouring the creamer in my coffee and was contemplating grabbing a bagel for what was technically my second breakfast when his deep voice startled me.

"Do you have something you want to tell us?"

I whirled around to see both Rue and Michael standing behind me, arms crossed, eyes pinning me to the spot I was standing. I blinked and set my coffee down.

"Um... no?" Looking between the two of them, I tried to fight through the lack of caffeine fog and figure out what the hell they were talking about. "Is there any reason you two are standing there like a grand inquisition is about to happen before I've even had my coffee?"

Michael held up his phone. "I just got word from a cousin of mine about the Hildago syndicate you asked me to look into. Do you know what this is?"

I leaned in to see a picture of me outside the safe house Simon had taken me to when I'd first met his team.

"I mean, it's a picture of me, obviously, but I don't know what you're trying to ask me, Michael." The lack of coffee and the aggressive way he was questioning me had my annoyance levels rising. "Why don't you cut with the bullshit and just come right out and say it? Or are we going to pull a Stockholm again?"

Rue rolled her eyes and smacked him on the arm. "Knock it off, you tyran géant. Hannah doesn't need to explain anything to us. She is our friend."

Michael had the decency to look apologetic. "I'm sorry Hannah, I didn't mean to come across like that. I'm not accusing you of anything, but you have to tell us what went down between you and the Hildago syndicate, because word came down from some of the big bosses." He paused, seeming to hesitate, as if he couldn't understand it. "There's been a hit put out on you. A massive one."

"Oh great. Someone wants me dead. What's new?" I sighed and took a sip of my coffee. This wasn't the best news, but it wasn't the worst either. It was just confirmation of what I already expected to hear.

Michael shook his head. "You don't understand. They've sent out word to all their associates. Basically, anyone that they've done business with or who owes them a favor will be gunning for you. The bounty is massive. They've called in their favor from my familia. So, I need to know, what exactly did you do to get on their bad side? Because I don't know if I can stop this."

I swallowed, my stomach that had been rumbling just a minute ago now hollow for different reasons. Fuck, fuck, fuck. This was bad. This was really bad.

"I caught them red-handed in a human trafficking ring. We were getting ready to put away José Hildago for life."

Michael swore and turned around. Rue just stared at me with eyes wide and filled with fear. "Oh, ma chérie. Why? Why would you ever try to go after José Hildago? Why did your superiors let you do this?"

I glared at them. "Because he's a sick, abusive, murdering, psychopath! There were babies and pregnant women in those cargo containers! Babies! If I didn't get justice for those innocent people, then who would? Huh? Do you think those families who are wondering what happened to their children, their mothers and their fathers, if they will ever get a chance to see them again, have the means or ability to pay for people like you to get justice for them?" Rue flinched and the muscles in Michael's shoulders visibly tightened.

"No, mercenaries" I spat the word out. "Aren't a luxury people like that can afford. All they have are people like me. People who just want to see some sort of justice served and wrongs righted. So yeah, I went after José Hildago and let me guess, little mister who can't get it hard unless it's with an underage girl, decided to take that personally and had his daddy sick his hounds on me."

Michael stayed perfectly still for a moment and then he slammed his fist onto the top of the island so hard I thought he might have cracked it, before storming towards the entryway and slamming the door closed behind him.

I blinked in the direction of his retreating back before turning back to Rue who was staring at the view of the city from where we were standing in the kitchen, a worried expression on her face. "Was it something I said?" I blurted the words out in a belated attempt at humor and was rewarded with a slight quirk of her lips upward.

"Michael will get over it. He's not upset with you, Hannah. He's just upset that he's out of control of the situation right now."

I sighed, regretting that I'd lost my temper with the only two friends I had at the moment. "I'm sorry Rue. I know you guys have no control over the contracts you take. I shouldn't have tried to make this about you guys. It was stupid to go after José without a better game plan." The beginnings of a tension and caffeine headache started to dance around my temples. When would this all stop? When I was dead? Now I had nearly the entire criminal underground of the east coast gunning for me and God only knows who else. I was a sitting duck, and it was only a matter of time before someone took me out. Michael and Rue were great, but with Evan and Simon gone, the chances of me being protected at all times were slim. Not to mention, I'd brought this to their doorstep, and I didn't want them getting hurt because of me. I closed my eyes, trying to block out the thoughts and scenarios that were racing across my brain.

Rue came to stand in front of me and I opened my eyes to see her holding out a fresh cup of coffee. "You're our friend, Hannah. Whatever happens, we're in this together. Michael left because he's going to talk to his family to figure out what they can do on their end of the contract. If what you say is true, and you have evidence that could put José Hildago away for good, then that may work in your favor. Like you said, he's a slimeball, and not respected in many of the underground circles. Not too many people would be upset if he was taken out."

I snorted and accepted the coffee from her. "So you're telling me that criminals have morals?"

She laughed and tossed me a wink as she walked back towards the table and her laptop. "Well, like the saying goes, there's no honor among thieves. But even thieves have their limits on how low they will go. José Hildago, his honor is lower than most. Just be patient. Wait for Michael and for word from Simon. We'll figure this out."

I stared at my coffee and turned her words over in my head. Sybil. Abromov. And now the Hildago Syndicate plus all their friends. There might not be honor among thieves, but there was among friends. And right now, I was sitting in a safe place with a giant target on my back. A target that was going to draw attention to anyone that was associated with me.

The picture of me outside the safe house that

had been sent to Michael's phone flashed through my mind. No matter what I did or where I went, these people were capable of finding me. Just like Sybil had been able to text me and seemed to know what I was doing at all times.

My fingernails tapped on the rim of my coffee cup as a plan took shape. I looked over at Rue who was absorbed in whatever program she was working on, and set my mug down on the counter before making my way to the front door and private elevator. I didn't have all the details of my plan fully fleshed out yet, but I knew two things for sure. I was going to need to leave the penthouse, and I was going to need a new ride.

Stepping into the elevator, I hit the button that would take me down to the garage level, and said a silent prayer of thanks that Evan had shown me where he kept the keys to his Audi. I might have only had two steps to my plan thought out, but that was ok. I was done running from the monsters that were after me and if I wasn't able to hunt them anymore, then I would do the one thing they wouldn't see coming. I was going to let them catch me.

CHAPTER THIRTEEN

Hannah

The scent of luxury leather in Evan's Audi RS7 surrounded me as I wove in and out of the Atlanta rush hour traffic. The rumble of the powerful engine and the smooth way it responded to my slightest touch thrilled me on a whole different level. I'd always loved cars, luxury cars especially, but had never had the opportunity to really appreciate them first hand. The only vehicle even close to luxury where I'd grown up had been someone's supercharged pickup truck. If it didn't have mud on the tires or the ability to haul a two-ton trailer, it wasn't considered valuable.

My fingers glided over the leather steering wheel and excitement shot through me as I saw a moment to break away from the traffic and hit the accelerator. The car leapt forward like a cheetah, the rumble of its engine vibrating through me, and I remembered Simon's words about riding that edge of chaos while being in complete and total control. That's what this was. Chaos and control. It was addictive. A girl could get used to this.

"Evan, you are so not getting this car back." I didn't even have to look in the rearview mirror to know I had a shit-eating grin on my face.

Sybil's old townhome came into view and I pulled into a parking spot across the street from it. The last time I'd been here Simon had kissed me on the doorstep and then minutes later I'd been left a present and reminder of the hell Sybil had put me through as a kid. I wasn't sure if there would be any surprises waiting for me this time, but I knew that whatever game Sybil was playing with me, the clues to it would be inside.

Bracing myself for whatever came, I covered my hair with a ball cap, hid my face with sunglasses, and pulled my weapon I'd stashed in a hidden compartment out to tuck it into the waistband of my jeans. I knew I was being followed and watched at all times, although I didn't know if they'd been able to track me to the team's penthouse. After the picture of me at the safe house, though, I wasn't taking any chances.

There was a chill in the air that hadn't been there before as I stepped out and hurried towards the entrance. It had been weeks since I'd been back here and the reasonable part of my brain tried to convince me that there was no way it wasn't already rented out and that I was about to crash someone's dinner. But as I turned the key I'd removed from under a hidden stone and listened to it click in the doorknob, I knew that wouldn't be the case. There was no way Sybil would ever give up something she considered to be hers, even if it was just an empty townhouse. I bet if I asked Rue to look into it, she would have found the house leased under a layer of shell companies that tied back to the Abromov group.

I stepped into the small foyer and, as if by muscle memory, reached for the light switch on the wall and stopped in shock at the sight that greeted me. Hanging from thin lines of string were hundreds of polaroid pictures. Each one different. Each one of me. And each one had my face crossed out in bright red angry slashes of ink. Me outside the agency headquarters. Me stopping for coffee at my favorite coffee shop. Me laughing at something Rue had said on a random shopping trip we'd taken just before leaving for Stockholm. Me standing outside this very townhouse, lips pressed against

Simons, hands clinging to his chest as if I wasn't sure I wanted to bring him closer, or push him away. I moved in and out of each picture and began to shake. There were older pictures too. Pictures of me at college. Of me with friends on a random bowling night. Of me out on one of my many failed dates. There were so many pictures they began to bleed together and I felt like a weight was crushing my chest, my throat closing as breathing became harder and harder. I dropped to my knees on the white living room carpet.

Why? Why had she done this? I couldn't understand it.

"You're MY Hannah."

Her voice. It slid through my mind like a serpent in the grass. How many times had she told me that? How many times had I brushed it off as just a silly phrase she used to say she loved me? But she never actually said she loved me, did she? For Sybil, it was always about ownership. About what she considered hers. I looked up at the dangling photos and stood up. No matter what happened, Sybil would never let me go. She considered me hers. Her personal plaything. And when my parents had threatened to send her away, to essentially take away her favorite toy? She'd straighten up, put on the fake niceness and charm until no one remembered how cruel and ugly she really was on the inside. But it was always there, just waiting for the day she finally felt like no one could stop her from letting her true nature shine.

A low whistle came from my left and I whirled around to see Abrams standing in the doorway, his too tall frame taking up most of the space in the small entryway. He, too, wore a low ball cap to hide his features. His bland tan jacket and dark denim jeans were nondescript enough that even with his height, no one would be able to identify any distinguishing features. His gaze danced from picture to picture for a moment and then back to me.

"Seems like you have an admirer."

I snorted and began to take down the images one by one. "More like a case of sibling rivalry taken to the extreme."

He cocked his head, looking at one particular picture that had captured me in a moment of pure joy. The one and only time my parents had taken us to the beach in Florida for vacation. I thought Sybil had stayed back at the hotel that day because she was sick. But evidently, she'd just been playing out whatever fantasy she'd had in her head with me. It was on that vacation that I'd decided wherever I lived, I wanted to be near the ocean. And I'd given up that dream for her. I looked at my crossed out eyes for a moment and then snatched the picture down.

"What was so important that you couldn't speak to me over the phone, Ms. Kelly?" Abram's voice was pitched low, but his tone was neutral, giving away nothing of his thoughts.

"Where's Simon?" I continued to move through the room, collecting the photographs and pieces of my past, but I observed his expression carefully.

He smirked, but it didn't reach his cold eyes. "He's indisposed at the moment. I'm not normally a message boy, Ms. Kelly, but I'll make an exception, considering the circumstances. Is there something I need to tell him?"

"No. I was just curious." I flicked him a cocky grin. "Had to give you a little test, that's all."

His expression didn't change. "Well then, if you'll excuse me, I have other important meetings to get to." He began to turn away.

"What's the connection between the Abromov Group and the Hildago Syndicate?"

He paused, a glint of something flashing in his eyes, but he gave nothing away. "What makes you think there is a connection?" There was weight to his words that hadn't been there earlier, and I took a step towards him, my fists crumpling the Polaroids I'd taken down.

"When I found that shipping container full of trafficked immigrants, I thought at first it was just a regular container. But that's not true, is it? The markings on the side were in Russian." Ice-blue eyes barely blinked in response, but he cocked his head.

"Ms. Kelly, I'm sure shipping containers come from all across the globe. One container in Russian doesn't mean a connection. I think you're grasping at straws."

Anger flared. There was something here, and I knew it. "No, I don't think I am. I think I'm hitting the nail on the proverbial head, Colonel, or whatever your title is." I raised my fist full of polaroids. "All this shit started when my case went up in flames from stolen evidence. Evidence that would have locked away José Hildago for life and brought down a major human trafficking ring. Evidence that my sister stole. My sister, who just happened to be the queen bee of an international arms dealer who also specialized in creating and manufacturing chemical weapons systems." I opened my fist and looked down at my crumpled and disfigured face. "I know I'm not exactly the typical intelligence agent. But you can't tell me that there isn't a connection there. My sister stole those documents for a reason and I'm pretty sure it's because it was going to connect her group to the Hildago's." And the decision had been an easy one for her to make. Not only was she protecting her ass, she was taking out the one person in the world she couldn't completely control. Me.

I looked up to find Abrams staring at me with a stony face and, for a moment, I thought he was going to blow me off and deny my accusations. But then he broke out into a wide grin that revealed two deep dimples and a genuine smile that nearly took my breath away. Holy hell, what was with these international spies that made them all so damn attractive? Did they have a special punch you in the lady bits kind of sexiness as a recruiting requirement?

"I'm sorry, can you tone down the high beams please, bud? This isn't exactly a pleasant experience for me. I've literally been hunted, stalked, and nearly assassinated twice now. I just want to put an end to it and figure out what the fuck is going on."

He chuckled. "My apologies Ms. Kelly. Have you considered my proposal from earlier?"

"Why, Colonel Abrams, I didn't realize this was a job interview." I intoned dryly.

"Everything is an interview and assessment, Hannah." His face schooled into a serious expression and I realized we were back to all business. "I can't tell you everything I know without some assurance."

I sighed and crossed my arms. "I'm tired of the games, Jonathan." I used his name just as he'd used mine, emphasizing it in my impatience. "I've literally got the entire east coast criminal underground hunting me right now and you're telling me you can't give me the information I need because I'm not part of your secret club?"

He shrugged, no hint of remorse in his expression whatsoever. "You're very intelligent and resourceful. What more could I, or my organization, offer you that you haven't already figured out?"

I paused, studying him for a moment as I analyzed his words. The words he was saying out loud and the ones he wasn't.

"Ok Abrams, give me your best recruiting pitch. But I can tell you right now, there better be a fantastic benefits package or I'm out. Don't try to bullshit me on this one."

He grinned and once more I was reminded of a predator baring its teeth. "I don't think you'll have an issue with the benefits, Ms. Kelly. In-fact, I think you'll find we have an excellent dental plan."

CHAPTER FOURTEEN

Hannah

Michael and Rue were once again waiting for me when I arrived back at the penthouse after my meeting with Abrams.

I cringed when I walked into the living room and interrupted what was obviously a heated discussion between them. Michael had his typical scowl settled over his features, his dark eyes locked onto Rue with a burning intensity that was simultaneously full of heat and frustration. Rue was standing a few feet away with her hands on her hips as she leaned in towards him with a matching scowl and stubborn set of her jaw. I glanced between the two of them and wondered for a split second if there was a possibility they'd be too distracted to notice me sneaking past them, but as if they were one, both of their angry stares transferred to me and I had to fight the feeling that I was a teen caught coming in from a late night party.

I held up the bag of greasy street tacos I'd picked up on the way home. "Did you guys eat yet? I got tacos."

Rue just blinked, her liquid gold eyes flashing for a brief second. Michael stiffened, glancing at the paper bag and then back to me before he turned to Rue and gave her a look in that silent way they communicated that said, "You handle her because I might kill her." Before he stomped off to the kitchen and began rummaging around.

I glanced over my shoulder at him and then back to Rue. "Does he have something against tacos? A personal vendetta, maybe?"

Rue's eyes narrowed in his direction and then shook her head. "No. He's just doing the typical male thing where he doesn't know how to process his frustrations, so he's just going to grunt and break things." At her words, a pan slammed hard down on the counter and I flinched, but Rue just snarled in his direction. "Someone hasn't learned that not every problem can be solved by killing someone."

I observed Rue as she glared at him while he

moved around the kitchen, taking down plates, utensils and condiments for our tacos.

Moving to stand next to her, I pitched my voice low, but not low enough that Michael wouldn't have heard me if he chose to pay attention. "Have you tried a blow-job?"

"What?!" Rue sputtered and Michael stilled for a moment before continuing to set up the kitchen island for our late night dinner, but I noticed he moved a little slower and quieter. I shrugged and held the taco bag out to her.

"Well, it's just my experience that if a man's bad mood can't be solved with food, then a blow job will do the trick. And based on the 'murder anything that moves' vibes that he's projecting, I'm going to guess that you're way beyond the food stages. Man is definitely backed up."

Rue's jaw hung open as she looked at me like I'd just grown two heads, but then she took the bag of tacos from me, muttering, "There's no way that's a thing...." Then trailed off into unintelligible French before moving toward the kitchen island and setting it down. But I didn't miss the heated and curious way she snuck looks at Michael as he prepared a homemade guacamole with the ingredients he'd taken out of the fridge.

I pulled out a stool and sat next to Rue as she

took out the tacos and portioned them out to the three of us. For a moment, I felt a sense of peace, like this was just a normal evening meal shared with friends. As if all the worries and the heavy weight of the information I'd gathered tonight were a problem for some other person and some other life-time. But then Rue pinned me with a pointed glare. "You know you're being hunted by two international criminal organizations, right?"

I took a bite out of my taco and groaned. There was nothing on this earth that tasted better than a fried to perfection tortilla stuffed with flavor explosions of carne asada and pico. I realized I'd gotten lost in the taste when I opened my eyes from my blissed out state to see both Michael and Rue glaring at me.

Reluctantly, I set the taco down on the plate Michael shoved under me and sighed. "Yeah, I know. But before you say anything, I was careful. I had to meet someone who could get me the info I needed. And I can guarantee you they would have made sure I wasn't watched or followed."

Michael arched a brow and scoffed, "Hannah, they caught you outside of our safe house. What makes you think they wouldn't have been able to follow you from here or back?"

I smiled, "Because the person I was meeting just

happened to be Jonathan Abrams, and if the head enforcer of the Enigma group can't keep a tail off my ass for a couple of hours, then I'm not sure I want to consider his proposal."

Rue pulled the guacamole to her and began to pile it on her plate next to a handful of tortilla chips. "What proposal? You mean joining the Enigma team?"

I nodded and took another bite, swallowing before I answered. "Yes, partly. But before we talk about that, I need to know what Michael's familia is willing to do about the hit on me. Did you get a chance to talk to them?"

Michael crossed his arms across his massive chest, looking for all the world like the Italian version of the incredible hulk and nodded. "It's complicated, but I think we've managed to work out an agreement. The fact that you have evidence that could put José Hildago in federal prison didn't help."

"What? But I thought they would want him out of the way!" I straightened in my stool, worry clawing at me. My plan hinged on Michael's familia and the other criminal syndicates backing off just long enough to allow me to have room to breathe.

"They do. They just also don't want him spilling any information in a plea deal that could see them ending up in the cells next to him." Michael finally seemed to relax and inhaled the tacos in one bite. I tried not to pout when he grabbed the last one, but I couldn't complain since I'd eaten six myself.

"So what's their solution, then? I don't care if they want to go after José for other reasons. I just need them to back off me for a while so I can handle what I need to."

Rue turned to me, "And what, exactly, do you need to handle?"

I gave her a cheeky grin and winked. "It's a secret."

She frowned. "Hannah, this is serious. You're taking a lot of risks right now. Do you really think it's smart to leave the people who can help you out of the loop?"

I reached out to grab her hand and gave it a squeeze. "Rue, I promise I'm not doing this intentionally, but right now, it's best that you don't know what's happening. I'll fill you both in when the time is right. But for now, I need you to trust me." My eyes pleaded with her. Her words from the other night about trust echoed through my mind. I needed her to have that trust in me now.

She searched my gaze for what seemed like a long moment and then gave me a soft smile. "You and Si really are peas in a pod. Perfect for each other. He doesn't like to fill us in on his plans until the last minute, either."

I leaned away from her with a grin. "Well, who do you think I learned it from?" Turning back to Michael, I leveled him a serious stare. "Ok, so what does your old man want in exchange for turning down the kill contract?"

It was Michael's turn to look serious. "That's the thing, Hannah, they can't turn it down. If they do, it will look bad on their reputation and the agreements they've made with other syndicates. The best they can do is put the word out quietly that they aren't heavily invested in the contract. But should someone want to chase the bounty, they won't stop them."

I sighed, crushed at the news Michael had just shared. They might not be willing to actively hunt me down, but they weren't willing to stop it from happening, either. Things were not looking very good so far. But I still had to try. "Ok, well, it's something, at least. What do they want in exchange for their lack of encouragement in my assassination?" The sarcasm dripping from my tongue couldn't be helped. Because really, that's all they were guaranteeing me.

"They want José Hildago removed from the equation, permanently." Michael's expression was blank, giving me no hint of what he thought about the situation, but the tense way Rue shifted in her seat gave me a clue as to what they'd been arguing about earlier.

"You mean they want you to remove him from the equation." I stated flatly.

"They want to draw him back into their fold by any means necessary, and this is just one more way they can dig their claws into him." Her eyes flashed a molten gold and her full lips curled into a snarl. "I will not allow this to happen."

Michael turned his gaze to her and looked like he was about to argue, but I interrupted him. "Well, it's a good thing he won't have to go through with it."

They both whipped their heads back around to me. "What do you mean?" Michael's voice was cautious and questioning, as if he wasn't sure he wanted to hear the answer.

"Because I'm going to be the one to take out José Hildago."

CHAPTER FIFTEEN

Hannah

I was starting to regret thinking I ever wanted to be a Bond girl. The early morning air still had a chill to it and wouldn't warm up until the sun was up much later in the day. My feet, shoved into plain canvas Converse because all of my shoes and belongings were still back at my old apartment, were practically ice-blocks. I shifted and attempted to regain some feeling in my toes by wiggling them.

The nondescript sedan we'd driven into the stakeout place was parked a few blocks away so that it didn't draw attention to us. The area we were in wasn't used to seeing much vehicle traffic and, if there was any, they didn't stick around long. This was the kind of neighborhood that you drove through with the doors locked and windows rolled up because somewhere along the way Siri had made you take a wrong turn. But this was where Abrams said our target would be, and I knew I could trust his team to give me accurate information. I just prayed my numb toes didn't cause me to trip and fall if the guy made a run for it and I had to give chase.

I pulled my beanie down lower over my ears and tried to lean in closer to the scuffed brick wall of the alley I was hiding in. It was a delicate balance of trying not to touch anything too slimy or greasy while also staying as far in the shadows as possible. A soft French accent filled my hidden earpiece. "I see movement. Looks like your boy is getting ready to leave."

"Thank fuck. It's colder than witches titties in a copper bra out here. Is he alone?" I shifted and tried to peer as much as I could around the corner of the building I was hiding behind, but large, overflowing trash cans were slightly obscuring my vision. Luckily some of the shops that weren't boarded up and abandoned had working surveillance cameras, which Rue had tapped into so that she could provide me with an extra set of eyes from her laptop in the sedan.

"Can't tell yet. You forced me into this tiny little space without all my tech, so I only have my laptop and honestly, I'm not sure these cameras have been updated since the eighties." She paused. "Actually, I think they may just be dirty."

"I told you, a van would be way too suspect in an area like this. If he has anyone else tailing him, we'd stick out like a sore thumb. And I can't exactly wait for a cleaning service, Rue. I need to know if he's by himself."

There was another long pause. "He's alone, but he's gone back inside. It looks like he forgot something. You sure we should do this without Michael?"

I sighed, anxiety and nerves clawing at my belly. "Positive. If Michael gets involved, then it means technically his mob family is also involved. It doesn't matter how much Michael tells them to fuck off. Blood is blood."

While Michael had left to find out more information on who might have accepted the kill contract on me, I'd given Rue the basics of my plan. Not everything, but enough to convince her she needed to help to track down my old informant. The last time I'd seen Javier Sanchez, he'd lawyered up with one of the top defense attorneys in the state of Georgia. It had been his testimony that was going to tie all the evidence we'd found directly to José Hildago. But he'd clammed up and denied everything, which eventually led to him being released into immigration's custody and sent back across the border. However, thanks to the information Abrams had shared with me, I learned that Javier hadn't gone back to his country at all. He'd stayed right here in Atlanta, working for none other than José Hildago himself.

For a man who claimed to be heartbroken over the loss of his sister at the hands of José, he sure was quick to accept a paycheck from him. I needed to know why.

Rue's lilting voice filled my ear again. "Ok, we have definite movement now. He just turned east, heading towards the cross-walk."

"Perfect, just like Abrams' report said he would." I slid out of the alley but still clung to the shadow of the buildings next to me. Javier was on the opposite side of the street and a few yards ahead. With it being so early in the morning there weren't many people up and about or even awake yet, but I still had to watch where I placed my feet on the off chance I accidentally disturbed one of the many homeless that congregated to this area. Not only did I not want to take away what little rest they got, I didn't need them sounding the alarm to my presence.

Javier turned the corner, and I paused for a

moment before hurrying across the street to follow behind him.

"Hannah, I've lost visual." Rue's voice crackled through the earpiece.

"It's fine. He's doing exactly what Abram's people predicted he would. This guy's pattern of living is like clockwork. Just move into position and be ready for my signal." I huffed into the mic as I dodged broken bottles and trash that littered the sidewalk. Abrams hadn't just come to the table with a name and information on what this guy was possibly up to. I wasn't sure if the file his surveillance team had pulled for me was meant to only be helpful, or to show off how good their capabilities were, but it was impressive. They knew everything there was to know about this man's day-to-day activities, down to the time he brushed his teeth for bed at night. When I made a quip about knowing the color of his underwear, Abrams had merely cocked a brow and flipped the page to reveal an itemized list of the man's personal belongings. He hadn't looked amused when I asked which person on his surveillance squad had taken one for the team and slept with the guy.

Still, it was impressive, and it was paying off in a big way. Because just like his file had indicated, he was heading right for a package store less than a half mile from his home. It was where I knew he would pick up his assignment from José for the day, or if there was nothing for him to do, he'd buy a case of beer and head back to his shitty house and drink himself into a stupor. Predictable.

Javier stopped outside the store, pulling a pack of cigarettes from the pocket of his dirty jeans and lit one, the puffs of smoke billowing into the cold air. I quickly slid into the shadows of derelict buildings and waited. Just as expected, at six o'clock on the dot, the fluorescent yellow open sign flashed on and the door opened with a jingle of bells. Javier flicked the butt of his half-smoked cigarette into the street and went inside. I stood perfectly still, my dark clothes blending in with the grime of the buildings, no longer bothered by the cold I'd felt earlier. This was it. We either cornered him here, or we lost this chance forever, and with it, my only hope to get answers.

I tensed as I heard the door bells jingle once more as Javier exited empty handed. Anticipation shot through me. This was even better than I'd expected. I peeled away from the shadows and followed him as he turned and headed towards an intersection where I'd knew he'd meet the morning bus. "Rue, get ready."

"On it."

Just as Javier would have crossed the street and made his way to the next block, a patrol car zoomed past him and turned down the street, sirens blaring. A second one followed shortly, coming from the direction of the major intersection. They pulled up short at the package store and came out with guns drawn. Javier turned around, eyes wide with panic, and watched as the officers entered the store with raised voices and shouted orders. Then he quickly broke out into a run, booking his way down a small alley between a row of dilapidated houses. I took off after him.

"Here he comes, Rue."

Tires squealed as Rue brought the sedan to a screeching halt at the end of the alley. Javier stopped short, tripping over himself in his panic and fell to waste covered ground. He scrambled, trying to regain his footing in the sludge.

I didn't have time to think about what was rotting beneath us as I slammed my knee into his back, driving him further into the dark filth. He grunted, a string of curses echoing off the narrow walls of the alley, and struggled to regain his footing even as I was wrenching one of his arms behind his back. He flopped around like a fish in the muck with me straddling his back like I was caught in some weird fish bucking rodeo. The oily slick that now covered most of his body caused me to slip to the side and ended up half on my side, one leg thrown over his back to maintain my seat. I was sure rodeo clowns had it easier than me at this point. Javier bucked hard and now it was my turn to curse as I felt the sludge splatter across my face.

"Listen here, asshole, stop flopping like a dead fish or I'm going to shove your face so far deep under this mud you'll grow gills."

That didn't seem to calm him down and instead he began flopping harder. But by this point, I'd regained some control and dislodged his other arm from beneath him. Wrenching it back to meet the other end of my cuffs, I snapped them in place and then slammed him hard into the ground, his head making a sick crack against the brick before he went limp beneath me. I took half a second to check and make sure he was still breathing before I got to my feet and looked down at my ruined Converse with a frown and resisted the urge to kick the unconscious man in the ribs. "My shoes are ruined now, asshole."

Rue called from the car, "I popped the trunk, let's get the package delivered and out of here Hannah."

"Yeah, yeah I'm coming. Next time we do this

I'm sitting in the car and you're doing the chasing down shit filled alleyways."

She snorted, "Please, mon chéri, I saw the way you ran him down. You enjoyed that more than you're letting on."

I grinned and looped an arm under Javier, who was coming around and mumbling groggily in Spanish, hauling him to his feet before guiding him to the open trunk just to shove him inside and slam it closed as he began to shout once more. "Maybe, but I'm still going to complain about it. And I'm putting a new pair of shoes on your tab."

She chuckled and then wrinkled her nose as I slid into the seat next to her. "Mon Diou, put it on Simon's tab. And not just the shoes. You need a whole new outfit now. You stink."

CHAPTER SIXTEEN

Hannah

I tapped the tall fresh pour of Guinness that sat in front of me and sighed. After Rue and I had brought our haul into the penthouse garage, a furious Michael had greeted us. But once I'd let him in on some of the information that Abrams had shared with me and popped the trunk to reveal Javier inside, he'd changed his tune and gave me a begrudgingly respectful, "Nice work."

As much as I'd wanted to head upstairs to shower and burn my clothes and shoes, there was still work to be done. After several hours of interrogation where I got to see firsthand just how creative Michael could get with his techniques, and was splashed with a few more pints of bodily fluid, I finally slipped away with the answers I needed.

Answers that, no matter how much I'd scrubbed and cleaned my skin, still left me feeling sick and dirty with the knowledge I now carried.

Moisture beaded on the outside of the glass and I watched it slip down the side of the pint glass as I let thoughts that were as dark as the ale it held carry me away. I didn't even notice when a dark shadow slipped onto the bar stool next to me until a silky voice rumbled low in my ear.

"Aye, lass, that's a fine pint you're letting go to waste."

I whipped my head around, startled to see Simon's dark gray orbs twinkling in the low lighting of the local Irish pub of the Buckhead Village district. It had been just a short walk from the penthouse to the bar that was a popular hangout for locals. I'd messaged for Abrams to meet me here to go over what I'd learned, so seeing Simon in his place was a complete surprise. But a pleasant one and it took everything in me not to launch myself at him in relief.

"What are you doing here?" My voice must have held some of the emotion I was trying to contain, because he frowned slightly and leaned forward to cup my jaw.

"What's happened, Hannah? Are you ok? Are you hurt, lass?"

His concern and the way he scanned me, assessing every inch of me, made me melt, and I gave him a soft smile. "I'm fine, Si. Should probably get an updated tetanus shot but, I promise, I'm not hurt."

He cocked his head, the frown not leaving his face. "Ok, what's the problem, then? Why are you meeting Abrams?"

I couldn't tell if he was jealous or just asking an innocent question. "What are you doing here, Simon? I thought you were away on a mission for Abrams."

He signaled the bartender and ordered a pint for himself. "Aye, Abrams had some meeting with a Senator and sent me in his stead."

I arched a brow. "Want to try that again, Mr. Gallagher?" I could smell the bullshit just as clearly as I could still smell the stench from the alleyway on my skin.

He glared at me for a moment, and then his lips twitched into a half-cocked smirk. "Ok fine, Jon doesn't know I'm here. I had a break in my assignment and Rue told me you were here meeting Abrams." He leaned forward then, the grin slipping from his face as he leveled me with a look that teased dark thoughts, and my breath caught as I felt a hand slip up my thigh. "And here I find you.

Fucking hell Hannah, give me one good reason I shouldn't haul you off to the bathroom, peel those jeans off your body, and fuck you until you can't see straight for going off on a half-cocked mission today for some low-level intel."

I swallowed thickly as a heady wave of lust flooded through my body at his words and the images they created in my mind. My voice dropped to a husky whisper, and I licked my lips, noting how his eyes flicked to watch. "You know damn well that wouldn't be a punishment."

His white teeth flashed a predatory smile, and he leaned in closer, the heat of his body and his scent enveloping me. "It would be if I didn't let you come."

My eyes widened. "You wouldn't."

His hand traced up my inner thigh, higher and higher, until it reached the junction between my legs, pressing against the exact spot where my jeans were rubbing against the sensitive flesh. I was sure by the flash of delight in his eyes that he could feel the wetness that was already beginning to build. "Aye, lass, I would. I would tease, taste and devour you until you were right on the edge and the entire bar heard you begging for your release. And then I'd leave you to think about what you've done."

I scooted forward slightly, trapping his hand

between my legs and leaned in to trace my lips against his jaw and whispered against his ear. "You might bring me to the edge, and you might make me scream and beg, but you and I both know, Simon Gallagher, that there's no way you could walk away from me without giving me your release, and mine." And then I slipped off my stool as my teeth nipped the lobe of his ear. "Excuse me, I think I need to use the ladies' room."

I moved through the crowd without looking back and was rewarded with a growl in my ear just as I reached the back of the bar. "You're a fucking she-devil, Hannah Kelly." And then the next thing I knew, he was gripping me by the back of my neck and pulling me towards a janitor's closet before opening the door and plunging us both into darkness.

I didn't know what my back hit, but I didn't care as suddenly his mouth and hands were on me and the taste consumed me and the feel of him. His lips stole my breath away even as his hands left my skin burning with his touch. I couldn't get close enough and ripped at the buttons of his jeans to bury my hand inside to grip the hard length of him, even as he'd gotten one leg of my pants down enough that I could slip it free.

I felt his teeth on my nipple as his hands ripped

my bra down and I groaned, arching into him. Then he lined the head of his cock up with my wet opening, pausing to coat it in my slickness as his tongue teased a line from neck to my jaw. "Is this what you wanted, Hannah? Tell me, lass."

"Yes, Simon," I moaned as he buried himself inside of me, filling me and then drawing back out to do it all over again. "Please." I felt his hands grip my ass cheeks as he held me against the cold wood and set a punishing pace. It didn't take long before I felt the first tingling awareness of my release as I tightened against him and as if he could sense without me saying a word that I was getting close, his hand slipped between us, his thumb rubbing against the slickness of my clit, driving me over the edge. I screamed, and he captured it with his mouth covering mine as I felt him harden, spilling over the edge into bliss with me.

Slowly, as our breathing and our heart rates came down, he let me go and then, with a gentleness that contrasted his earlier brutality, cleaned the mess we'd made with a handkerchief he'd pulled from his pocket. I snickered when I saw it in the dim light of the closet, thinking of how, when I'd first heard about him, I had the impression of a posh aristocrat with an ascot and cane. Seeming to read my thoughts, his eyes twinkled, and he tucked back into his pocket. "Do you have a problem with my 'kerchief?"

I shook my head as he lifted my foot and drew my jeans back up, his hands tenderly tracing the contours of my leg. "No, I enjoy seeing this gentlemanly side of you."

He stood then, righting his own clothing, and leaned down to place a soft kiss on my lips. "You have a way of bringing out both sides of me, love."

A pounding knock sounded at my back, startling me as I realized I was leaning against the closet door. Just as I thought we were about to be exposed to the whole bar, a familiar voice sounded through the thick wood. "If you two are done, I believe I have a meeting with Ms. Kelly."

"A meeting with a Senator, huh?" I cocked a brow and moved away from the door as Simon opened it to see Abrams standing in the small alcove holding both our pints of Guinness. Simon, for his part, didn't look phased, just smiled darkly at his handler, but I noticed how he positioned himself slightly in front as if he wanted to protect me from whatever tongue lashing or judgement we were about to receive.

I scooted around him and grabbed one pint from the Colonel's hand. "Oh, thanks Jon, I worked up a thirst." Then tipped my head back and downed half the pour with a satisfied sigh. "About time you got here. Should we go sit down, though? Kind of exposed out here and we've got things to discuss." I turned away from both men, hiding a snicker at the shocked way Abram's jaw snapped shut and the devilish grin Simon gave him before he took his own pint and followed behind me.

"Fucking hell, Simon, you could have warned me." I heard growled low behind me, to which Simon just chuckled. "I told you she was a hellion, Jon. Better get used to it."

I glanced over my shoulder to see Jon give Simon an assessing look. "You know we don't do partnerships on the teams, Simon." Something about the way he said the words had me straining to hear the rest of the conversation as I wove in and out of the crowd to a table set away from the main bar.

Simon's voice was low, but I picked up three words that made my heart skip a beat. "You do now."

CHAPTER SEVENTEEN

Simon

When Rue filled me in on the events of the past twenty-four hours, it filled me with a sick combination of rage and worry. I was torn between going after Abrams and beating him to a bloody pulp for sending Hannah off on her own on what I was sure was some bloody test to find out if she had what it took to join one of his Enigma teams, or chasing her down and seeing for myself if she was ok or not. It only took me half a second to decide and when I walked into the pub, I knew I'd made the right choice. Her face held every thought as if she was an open book and I could see the inner turmoil that she'd learned today was causing her. It made me want to kick Abram's ass even more. There was no reason for him to send her on that mission because

I was sure that whatever Javier had told her in their interrogation, Abrams already knew and had a source for. What had happened today was literally just a trial by fire.

Still, I knew that even if she'd had the information handed to her in a nice little packet, it wouldn't have made hearing it any easier. But I was curious about what she'd learned and how it tied into Sybil and the Abromov group. When I'd questioned Rue and Michael, they'd merely exchanged one of their looks and said that I would need to talk to Hannah about that. Whatever they'd uncovered, they felt like it was personal to Hannah, and only she was the one who could really share the complete picture.

Hannah slid into a secluded booth, and I followed behind her. Technically, this wasn't my mission anymore and Hannah wasn't my asset, but I would be damned if I let her face off with Abrams by herself again. The man was a wolf on his best day and an absolute monster on his worst. He might have been one of the good guys, but good was only shades of grey when it came to what he deemed beneficial to the Enigma group and those they answered to. If I was mission oriented, Jonathan Abrams was mission obsessed.

Abrams took the seat across from us and turned

to Hannah. "Well, what did you learn?"

Hannah just smiled and turned to me. "He doesn't waste time, does he?" She turned back to him. "Tell you what, how about you show me yours and I'll show you mine?"

Jon didn't blink. "I believe I've already shared plenty with you. You found Javier exactly where I said he'd be, correct?"

She nodded. "Oh yeah, he was there like a nice pretty package, all wrapped up for me. But you know, maybe I'm finally learning not to trust anyone in this business because that just didn't sit right with me. You made it too easy, Jonathan."

Abrams arched a brow, the only sign that Hannah might have been on to him. "So, are you going to tell me what you learned? Or do you have more questions for me?"

Hannah sat back and glared at him. "You're a cold mother-fucker Jonathan Abrams. Do you know I ruined my favorite pair of Converse in shit filled alleys when you could have just told me what I needed to know?" She sighed, as if resigning herself that trying to get any empathy from Abrams was going to be like trying to wring water from a rock.

"Fine, you win. I hope I passed your fucking test though, because this will be the last time you make me run down an informant without cause."

Pride welled, and it took every bit of self-control I had not to kiss her senseless right there. I cleared my throat instead and placed a hand under the table on her thigh, willing her to know through my touch that I supported her.

"Well, now that we've established that you both know what the fuck is going on, would either of you care to fill me in?"

One set of green and one set of blue eyes turned to me, almost as if they'd been so locked in their silent battle of wills they'd forgotten I was there.

Hannah glanced back at Abrams. "You mean he doesn't know?"

I frowned. "Know what?"

Abrams shrugged. "It wasn't necessary to fill him in. The development had nothing to do with his mission involving the Abromov group."

I looked back and forth between the two. "Excuse me, but know what?"

Hannah turned to me and the darkness I saw her battling earlier was back in her gaze. "The Abromov group wasn't just involved in weapons dealing. When I found that shipping container of immigrants, I thought I was just busting up a human trafficking ring. What I didn't realize at the time is that the Abromov Group and the Hildago Syndicate were working together on a new venture project." She frowned. "When we raided their offices, we took some information that would have linked the two organizations together. I didn't see it. But Sybil knew and that's when she decided I needed to be removed from the picture.

She picked up her half drunk pint and took a few more swallows, as if to steady herself.

"Javier wasn't a heartbroken brother mourning his sister, he was a plant. I told Sybil everything — well, mostly everything. But she knew I was working on a major human trafficking case. It didn't take much for her to realize who I was going after." She stared into the depths of her Guinness with a look that spoke volumes. It was of utter betrayal. She'd confided in her sister as if she was someone to be trusted, but Sybil had never deserved or earned that trust. She'd always been out for her own selfish gain.

I turned to Abrams. "What do you know about the project that the Abromov group was working on? Why did they want to partner with human traffickers?"

Abrams hesitated, his gaze flicking back and forth between me and Hannah before he seemed to come to a conclusion and cleared his throat. "The Abromov Group used weapons dealing to fund their other activities. It was never about selling weapons. Their primary focus was always about the sciences."

Hannah looked up and nodded. "Yes, that's what always confused me about Sybil's involvement. Selling weapons just seemed so low class for her. I never understood it until I realized the connection between the two criminal groups."

She turned to me. "Have you ever heard of a South African scientist nicknamed 'Dr. Death'?"

I frowned. "I'm somewhat familiar. He was a part of a genocidal program during apartheid, correct?"

Abrams nodded. "You're correct. The project, named Project Shore, committed unspeakable atrocities against the South African people. The program that this 'Dr. Death' headed up involved chemical and biological weapons that were supposedly meant to be used for mass crowd control. They were mind altering and physically incapacitating drugs that would make an entire population pliable and weak against armed forces."

"When we were interrogating Javier, he couldn't tell us much, which is typical of someone at his level. All he said, over and over, was that the new Dr. Death would come for us." Hannah's green eyes bored into mine. "And that this new Dr. Death, is Sybil."

CHAPTER EIGHTEEN

Hannah

I looked down at the frail hand clasping mine. The blue of her veins was a stark contrast to the porcelain tone of her skin. The family had taken their turns saying goodbye over the past several days. It was her wish. "I don't need ya'll standing over me like some sick death watch. I know I'm dyin'. Don't need to be reminded of it by your sorry faces." But I was the only one who kept showing back up, and for as much as she fussed at me, she never turned me away.

The firm but gentle squeeze was all I needed to know she'd woken up from her brief nap. She did that more and more every day. I wasn't sure which day I'd show up to find her drifted away into that final dark sleep.

"Hannah, you've got to get out of here." Her voice was

soft. Softer than I'd ever heard it before, and for a moment I wasn't sure I'd even heard her correctly.

"I ain't goin' nowhere, Memaw. I'll be here as long as you need me." I picked at the bright crochet blanket I'd brought from her house. Mom and Dad had already packed up her little cottage and put most of her things in storage when she'd been moved to the hospice facility. But I knew she'd loved the crazy, mismatched patterns of this afghan and I'd snagged it before they could box it up.

She chuckled, "Lord save me from stubborn Kelly women. You still ain't got the sense God gave a billy-goat. Now you listen here, girl, and you listen to good." The whip was back in her voice and I sat up a little, my eyes blinking back tears.

"You keep letting other people determine who you are. Especially that sister of yours. No one has to tell Sybil who she is. She knows. She just tries to hide it because if anyone looked behind the fake curtain long enough, they'd see she's been pullin' everyone's strings for longer than they want to admit." I gaped at her.

"Memaw! Sybil can be- difficult- but she's not evil."

My grandmother just snorted and shifted in her bed. I leaned over to help her adjust her pillow and when she was sitting more upright; she gestured to a glass of water on her bedside table. "No? Not evil? Maybe that's true." She took a sip and closed her eyes as if the effort to even do that had exhausted her.

"But she ain't good either." Her eyes opened again, and their watery blue pierced me like a cloudless summer day. "The darkness tries to hide the light. Remember that Hannah. Darkness and death go hand in hand. And if you keep letting your light get smothered by Sybil, you're going to eventually end up the same way."

"Memaw, you shouldn't say that about Sybil. She loves you and it would break her heart if she heard you talk like this." I frowned, not sure why my grandmother was so hell bent on trying to convince me that Sybil had some ulterior motive.

My grandmother looked at me for a long moment and then nodded. "And I love her, Hannah. Believe me, I've spent the past decade trying to understand her. But just like I can tell you that sometimes you're as slow as a molasses on a winter day, I can also say that the only thing your sister loves is control. One day you'll wake up and realize it." She waved a hand. "Now go on, I need to sleep."

I watched as Simon processed the information we'd just shared with him. I knew what he was thinking. Had Tory known about this? Had she been ok with the Abromov group testing experimental drugs on humans? He didn't voice anything, just turned back to Abrams. "If this is true, and Sybil and the Abromov are dealing with chemical and biological weapons testing, this would take priority over every other objective."

Abrams nodded in agreement. "You would normally be correct. However, when Ms. Kelly went after José Hildago, the operation came to a stop. As far as we know, it hasn't started up again."

Simon turned his gaze back to me. "That's why the Hildagos are going after you."

I shrugged, "The Hildago's, the Abromov group, my sister. I'm a very popular girl at the moment."

He frowned and his fingers that hadn't left my thigh tightened. "This isn't funny, Hannah. Your sister is at the center of two international criminal organizations and is gunning for you. We already know her obsession with you goes beyond the norm. She's setting you up."

I leaned forward. "You don't think I know that? There's something my Memaw told me years ago, and I didn't realize how right she was until now. What's the one thing Sybil loves more than anything? It's not me. It was never about me. It's all about control."

When the pieces had clicked into place, a

picture of Sybil I'd never realized came into clear view. The taunting, the teasing, the manipulation. All of it was about control. She never hated me so much as that she just wanted to control me. And not just me, everyone around her. When we were kids, she used fear to control and get her way. When that stopped working, she played mind and emotional games.

It made sense that working with Abromov's group would appeal to her. To control and manipulate a whole population? Right up her alley. That kind of power was something only a true narcissist would want. And that's why she was so willing to walk away from me with her fake death. She'd found something that gave her a greater sense of control and fed that addiction in a way that I never could. But she had to play one last game with me, pull one last string, and so that's why she'd stolen the evidence in the Hidalgo case. It's why she'd orchestrated to plant Javier Sanchez as an informant. It's why she taunted me even now with her fake warnings and text messages.

He looked at me, searching and assessing for a moment, before he nodded. "Ok. So, what do you plan to do?"

I smiled and couldn't help the little thrill that

went through me that he acknowledged that I had a plan already. "It's pretty simple. I'm going to do what I've always done. I'm going to let Sybil get her way."

One dark brow arched in a curious expression, but he waited for me to elaborate. Abrams wasn't so patient, however, as he tapped the table and looked between the two of us, confusion settling between his brows. "I'm sorry, Ms. Kelly. Would you care to elaborate on that plan?"

I turned towards Abrams. "What would you do if I told you I could get you the head of not one, but two international criminal organizations and none of it would be tied back to you, the U.S. government, or anyone else?"

Abrams cocked his head, those ice-blue eyes darkening slightly and I could see the gears in his mind turning over my words, assessing and weighing them. "I'd say I would have no idea what you're talking about, Ms. Kelly. That criminal operations are a matter for the federal government and as I understand it, you no longer work in any official capacity for the Department of Justice. Now, if you'll excuse me. I feel like this meeting has officially ended and I have other matters to see about."

I grinned. "That sounds fantastic, Jonathan. But

before you leave, we need to discuss one more thing."

His jaw flexed, and he eyed me with suspicion. "And what's that?"

"I'm going to need a better dental plan."

CHAPTER NINETEEN

Hannah

Before Jonathan Abrams had slipped away into the night to make whatever secret deals he had in the works, he asked Simon for a private word. And with a frustrated glance back to me that told me just how little interest he had in whatever conversation they were about to have, Simon followed him out onto the street. I sat there in the booth by myself for a long a moment, the events of the past few days play over and over in my head.

I knew I'd promised Abrams that I could hand him the head of both the Hildago's and the Abromovs, but what I hadn't said was that I still wasn't sure how to pull it off. Something nagged at the back of mind like a broken record. For as much as I'd learned today from Javier and Abrams, there were still so many unanswered questions. I thought about the pictures I'd found hanging in Sybil's townhome. Maybe at the beginning of all of this I would have been disturbed, scared even. But now that I understood what and who my sister was, I could see the cycle she was repeating. Text me and warn me about a potential threat. Love bomb me into thinking we were the best of friends and my entire world revolved around only her. Bombard me with fear and use my worst nightmares against me. Then laugh and call me crazy when I'd run and tattle to Mom and Dad. Only this time, there was no running to Mom and Dad.

I sat up, a sudden thought taking root. A cycle. It was a cycle. Where had she'd said she'd gone before she was to leave for Stockholm? I replayed the memory of our last night before my entire world flipped upside down. And then it hit me like a ton of bricks. The last missing piece of my plan clicked into place and I pulled out the phone Michael had given me, shooting off a quick text. Then I stood up and slipped out into the night, not bothering to flag down Simon or Abrams. This was something that they couldn't help me with and if I was right, I was the only person who knew what Sybil's next move would be and I didn't have time to waste with all the logistics and planning those two would want to do.

Like clockwork, a text message appeared in my notifications as I made my way through the streets of the village district to the penthouse garage.

Unknown Number: I got your message.

Me: We need to talk.

Unknown Number: There's nothing to discuss. You interfered where you shouldn't have. Now you're paying the price.

Me: Sissy, please. I'll do whatever you want. Please, just help me.

Unknown Number: Can't your new friends help you? Or your new boyfriend? You don't need me.

Me: Simon and the team can't do anything about it. Their hands are tied. These people are going to kill me. I need you, Sybil.

I watched as bubbles appeared and disappeared on my screen. My stomach was doing somersaults as I waited for her response. Then finally it came.

Unknown Number: You never could fix your own problems. Meet me at the coordinates I'm sending now.

Me: Thank you, Sissy! I'm so scared.

Unknown Number: Just be there and come alone. I'll take care of it Hannah - just like I always do. I'm glad you finally realized that I wasn't the enemy.

Me: You were right, Sybil. I've been so selfish.

Unknown Number: It's ok. I forgive you.

A location appeared on the screen next, and I smiled grimly. She did exactly as I knew she would. Now I just had to be as predictable as possible in our cycle until her guard was down. It was the only way. I keyed in the code to the garage and headed for the Michaels blacked out Hummer. Where I was going, I would need a little more torque than Ethan's Audi could provide. Not to mention I was pretty sure Michael would have made sure his personal vehicle had all of his favorite bells and whistles like bulletproof glass and run flat tires. Because knowing Sybil, I was going to need them.

———

At about a half mile from my parents' house, I turned the headlights off on the Hummer. In the spring and summer, the trees that lined the road leading to the barn would normally hide any approaching vehicles. But it was fall now and on a clear night like tonight. Headlights could be spotted up to a mile away. I parked the vehicle about twenty yards from the barn doors and waited in the silence. I could see the lights of my parents' house a couple hundred feet away, but I couldn't tell if they were home or not. I hadn't spoken with them since I'd confronted them over Sybil. My mother's reaction and the way they'd glossed over her treatment of me had left me angry and confused. Parents were supposed to protect their children. All mine had done was enable my abuser to continue her behavior behind a fake smile and closed doors. Whatever attempts my father had made to warn me about Sybil had come years too late and I saw now that it was guilt that drove him to even attempt to talk to me about her.

Behind the barn I could make out the neighbors' corn fields. The rows and rows of cornstalks, almost ready for the fall harvest, had once been a childhood haven of safety for me. Sybil would never follow me into the soft soil and tilled up earth. It was where I ran when I couldn't make it to my grandmother's cottage. It was in those fields that I'd buried Daisy.

I exited the Hummer and approached the barn doors. It was dark and quiet. The only sounds I could hear were the crickets and the rustle of the breeze through the cornstalks. This barn was technically our neighbors, but we'd always been allowed to use it as a second storage place for our vehicles. I paused with my hand on the rough wood handle and listened, but there weren't any sounds coming from inside. A part of me worried I hadn't played my role well enough and that she'd spooked. But there was only one way to find out.

I entered the cool building that smelled of hay, engine oil, and dank earth. It was empty. My stomach sank. "Sybil?" I called out in the darkness, but only my voice echoed back. Fear and anxiety gnawed at me. Where was she?

A soft rustle had me shifting to the balls of my feet, ready to run or fight. All of my senses were on high alert as I waited. She had to be here. This was just another one of her tactics to throw me off my guard. Create an environment of fear and make me pliable to whatever she wanted. I reached for my back holster, where I kept my weapon tucked, fingers settling on the butt of my gun. Another rustle came from closer to me now and in the next breath, my gun was in my hand, my thumb flicking the safety off.

"Who's there?" I called out, my heartbeat pounding in my ears. Then suddenly around a stack of hay bales two green eyes, glowing in the darkness, blinked at me and let out a curious meow.

I let out a breath of air and half a laugh. It was one of the barn cats that roamed the farm and kept the rats and mice at bay. He turned and rubbed his body against the bale of hay, tail flicking as if to tease me for fearing a cat. I leaned down to give him a scratch under the chin and was rewarded with a rumbling purr before he flicked his ears suddenly and took off into the shadows. Frowning, I stood up to see what had spooked him when suddenly the world around me exploded in pain and blinding light. Then, everything went dark.

·····································

CHAPTER TWENTY

·····································

Hannah

Pain. That was the first thing I became aware of. My head felt like someone had used it as a piñata at a six-year olds birthday party. I started to panic when I opened my eyes to complete darkness, thinking for a moment that I'd gone blind from the blow. But as my senses came back to me, I realized it was dark because a cloth bag was covering my head. The next thing I noticed was the painful bite of handcuffs on my wrists. I was on the ground, that much I knew. The muscles in my back and shoulders groaned in protest as I tried to adjust my position. And based on the hardness I felt as I shifted, I must have been handcuffed to one of the barn poles.

Distant voices reached me, and I stilled.

Fighting off a wave of nausea, I tried to slouch down and appear limp once more. Whoever was speaking hadn't realized I'd woken up yet, and I wanted to keep it that way as long as possible. At least until I could get a clearer head and not want to gag with every little movement.

A thickly accented male voice came closer. He sounded agitated and angry, but I couldn't quite make out what he was saying. A softer, more feminine voice responded. She was cold, haughty, and condescending. *Sybil.* Anger and fear warred within me. I'd been so stupid to think she'd fall for my trick. More than that, I'd been so stupid to not tell Simon or anyone else what my plan was. When was I going to learn? Footsteps came closer, and I braced myself for whatever was coming. Reflecting on my mistakes right now would not matter. Clearly, it was too late to help.

"You were always a terrible actor, Hannah. I can tell by the shift in your breathing and the stench of fear coming off you that you're awake." Sybil's voice slapped at me and I flinched, wincing, as the bag was jerked off my head. She stood over me, blocking my view of anything else but her haughty face, but I could see there was something behind her. The barn was still fairly dark, only lit by a single oil lamp set in the middle of the earth-packed floor.

I blinked up at her, my vision still blurry from the blow to my head. "What do you want, Sybil?"

She gave me a grim smile and crossed her arms. "It's not what *I* want, Hannah. It's what *you* want. You asked me for help, remember?"

I shifted and felt a drip of something wet slide down the back of my neck. Was I bleeding? "I'm not sure that my idea of helping and your idea are the same things, Sybil. I'm a little fuzzy on the details, but I'm pretty sure I didn't ask to have my brain scrambled."

Sybil snorted and shook her head. "Oh Hannah, as much as I would have *loved* to take credit for that. I *did* come here to help you."

I blinked at her again and she must have read the confusion or the utter lack of interest in any of her mind fuck games because she rolled her eyes with an exaggerated sigh and turned to the side to reveal what was behind her.

And then I realized why I'd heard a male angry male voice earlier, because zip tied to a chair with a head that looked like mine felt, was none other than José Hildago himself. He was bloodied and bruised. The crisp white shirt and suit jacket he wore had been ripped to shreds. It looked like he'd been drug through hell and back, putting up a fight the entire way. I looked at Sybil, who was dressed as if she'd just stepped off the pages of a high society magazine. She definitely hadn't been the one who turned José into a personal punching bag, which meant that her armed guards were here somewhere.

"Umm... thanks?" I eyed José, whose face was so swollen and bruised I wasn't sure how he managed to see. "But if you were helping me, then how did José know I was meeting you here?"

Sybil smiled and walked back over to the man, grabbing a fist full of hair and yanking him back so hard that even I winced. Maybe she'd gotten a few licks in herself after all. "Because I told him, of course." The man moaned, and I could see that he was slipping in and out of consciousness. The light from the oil lamp lit up Sybil's face and a sick feeling roiled in my stomach. There was a look there that I hadn't seen since the day she'd gifted me the bloody parts of my mutilated puppy.

"Sybil... Sissy." I called to her softly, hesitantly. "You need to let him go."

Sybil said nothing for a moment, just watched as blood dripped down from a cut above his eyebrow.

"Did you know our parents tried to separate us?" Her voice, when she spoke, was barely above a whisper.

Shifting against the pole, I wiggled my fingers and wrists in the cuffs, testing their tightness. "Yes. Dad told me that after you threw Daisy to the dogs that if you ever did anything like that again, they'd send you away."

She laughed, cold, mirthless. "Is that what they told you? Of course, they did."

The handcuffs were tight, but not so tight that I couldn't rotate my wrist. I had to get out of them, but without the key or wire cutters, there weren't many options, and the only one I could think of was going to hurt like a son of a bitch. "What are you talking about? If there's a different version of the story, then let's hear it."

She whipped around. "You weren't supposed to *be here*, Hannah. Did you ever wonder why we look so much alike? Did you ever think that maybe it was because we're more than just sisters?"

My wrist ached as I twisted and turned my hands into position. I had to get her distracted, so she didn't notice the pain that I wouldn't be able to hide.

"No, we're Irish twins and we *are* sisters. You aren't making any sense."

She rolled her eyes. "The truth stares you in the face and yet you do nothing but see what you choose to see. We *are actual twins.* Not Irish or whatever made-up bullshit our parents told us. Fraternal twins."

I stilled, her words hitting me like a ton of bricks. "What the hell are you talking about, Sybil? That's impossible. Even more so, why would our parents lie about us being twins if we're actual sisters?"

"Because they separated us at birth and they didn't want anyone to know." She looked at me, her eyes so like mine, her face just only slightly more delicate, her features just a touch sharper. "We were adopted, Hannah. Only when they adopted us, they only adopted one of us. Me. You were adopted too, by another family, but something happened and the adoption never went through."

I forgot about the handcuffs and the half-dead man in the chair. I forgot about the pain thundering in my head and the metallic taste of blood on my tongue. "I'm adopted?"

"*We're* adopted. They didn't get you until you were almost four years old after a call from a foster agency."

I scoffed, sure she was lying at this point. "I knew you were crazy Sybil, but this is the biggest load of bullshit I've ever heard. We literally have pictures of us as babies in our parent's house."

"No!" she shouted. "We have pictures of *me* as a baby. Not you. Oh sure, there are pictures of us as little kids but none of us are together as babies. Not one."

"Well then, why would they change our birthdates? Or our ages?" None of it made sense, and the more I tried to piece the blurred edges of my memories together, the more confused I became.

She shrugged. "Honestly, because they didn't want to admit they'd had to adopt. Or that they had separated twins. What would the community think of them?" She said mockingly.

Closing my knees to my chest, and leaned my head back against the wooden pole, not caring about the sting of pain it caused. "I don't believe you."

"Believe what you want. It's the truth. And do you know when I found out?" She flicked a piece of hay off her shirt with a mild look of disgust. "I found out when they threatened to send me away. They had to report the adoption, and that they weren't my birth parents."

I opened my eyes again and stared at her. "That's when you changed."

She nodded, "Yes. When they realized I knew, they would do anything to keep me quiet." A grin spread across her face in twisted delight. "*Anything.*

Do you know why I stopped harassing you so much? Because I no longer needed to threaten them with hurting *you* to get what I wanted. I had something much better. The truth."

I shook my head. I knew my parents. Hiding an adoption? It was a possibility. My parents grew up in an era where some things you just kept quiet about. Especially in the South, where people talked and gossiped like it was the next thing to breathing. They probably didn't want that hanging over our heads as a stigma. I eyed Sybil, her grin stretched tight across her face as like the Cheshire Cat. Like a cat that had just caught the mouse and was fully enthralled in toying with it. Controlling it.

That's what this was all about. Control. And suddenly I knew what I had to do.

"Ok, Sybil. I believe you."

CHAPTER TWENTY-ONE

Hannah

She looked at me for a moment, her gaze clouded with suspicion, so I continued on. "But what I don't understand is why I'm still handcuffed to this pole and he," I pointed my chin towards the unconscious José,"...is zip-tied to a chair."

She smiled, but it didn't quite reach her eyes. "Hannah, what's the one thing I've always told you?"

I licked my lips, unsure of what to say next. "That I have terrible taste in men?" It was the only answer I could think of.

A short, barking laugh escaped her lips, and she moved closer to me, bending down so that we were at eye level, and for the first time, I saw in them the true depths of her madness. Her fingers gripped my jaw painfully as she leaned in closer. "That you're *my* Hannah. All mine. And no one gets to hurt you, harm you, or *control you*. Except me. We were destined from birth to be together and no one is going to take that away. Simon tried. Sergei tried. And now this pathetic boy is trying. *I will not let them.* "

Her hot breath fanned over my face, and it took everything in me not to recoil away from her. *Holy, fucking, psychopath.* When I got out of here, I was going to have a serious conversation with my parents about their enabling tendencies and maybe sign us up for family counseling. But I had to get away first and some instinct in me knew that there was a countdown clock somewhere ticking the seconds away.

"You're right, Sissy. No one can take that away. And I don't want them to, but- "I pointed over her shoulder with my chin. "His family is going to be looking for him. And I'm almost positive they are on their way here now, or about to be. You need to get these handcuffs off me so we can get out of here." She stood back up and scoffed at me.

"Let them come. I stationed my guards all around this property. They can handle whatever idiots the Hildago's send."

I shook my head. "No, Sybil, you don't understand. It won't just be the Hildagos. It will be every hitman they have on their contract list. Because they aren't coming after just José, they will come after *me*. You lured him here with the promise of taking me out. I know José Hildago. I know how egotistical and self-absorbed he is. He would absolutely jump at the chance to kill the person who dared to go after him." Sybil studied me, silently weighing my words. I pressed on.

"You know this too. It's why you set the trap for him. He may be stupid and hot-headed, but his family isn't, Sybil. They will have figured out he went by himself by now. They'll be on their way. And they will have sent every contract killer they know headed this way, too." I leaned forward, straining against my cuffs. "We need to get out of here."

I waited, praying silently that she heeded my warning, and just as I thought she was about to ignore me once more, an alert chimed from a small black radio she had tucked into the waistband of her pressed linen slacks. She clicked the receiver and mumbled a few words in rapid Russian. The man's voice on the other end was terse and clipped but, by the way, her gaze flicked rapidly from José and then back to me. I knew my calculated guess hadn't been too far off. She barked a few more orders and tucked the radio back inside her belt before pulling a set of keys from her pocket. And approached me.

"Well, it seems some of your training has paid off. You were correct. My men tell me there are vehicles approaching." She slipped the keys into the cuff and quickly released them, but didn't bother helping me to my feet. Just turned and walked back towards José.

I stood, rubbing my wrists and then rolling my shoulders as I tried to get the blood flow back into them. I didn't even have time to process what was happening when suddenly she pulled out a silenced 9mm handgun, pointed it directly at Josés head, and pulled the trigger.

"Sybil! What are you doing?" I cried out, stumbling backward as she whirled and pointed the gun directly at me.

"Taking care of loose ends. If what you say is true and the Hildagos are on the way here, then our business dealings are done, and they will come after me as well as you. Or maybe it's your little hodge-podge group of friends thinking they can steal you away. Either way, you're coming with me. No one is separating us again."

I held my hands up, pleading with her. "Sybil, no one knows I'm here. I didn't tell my friends where I was going. That *is* the Hildago's and you've just killed, literally, any chance we had of negotiating with them."

She gave me a grim smile and motioned with her gun toward the rear entrance to the barn. "Well, it's a good thing I have no intentions of negotiating with anyone. Move."

I stumbled forward, my head still fuzzy from the blow to it earlier and nausea coming in waves now that I was moving. The world felt like it was titled, spinning on the wrong axis as I moved, and just as I was about to reach the door, I heard the muffled shouts of men outside and the distinct sound of bullets hitting the side of the barn. Gunfire erupted behind us and I felt a body slam into me from behind. It was Sybil. We hit the ground hard and pain exploded in my head again as it bounced against the earth-packed floor. She groaned and then pushed herself off me before jamming the end of her gun into my ribs and screaming in my ear to get up.

I scrambled to my feet, unsure of who was shooting but not caring, because there was no way I was going to turn around and look. We burst through the doors and ran straight for the corn-fields. Shouts came from behind us, more bullets exploding into the crisp night air. My feet sunk into the mud and I heard Sybil curse as she stumbled behind me. I could hear the voices of Sybil's men as they barked orders and other voices, unfamiliar ones, screaming back at them.

When I paused to catch my breath and orient myself in the maze of corn, Sybil grabbed my shoulder and I felt the cold press of her gun on the back of my neck. "Keep moving."

I tensed. "Sybil, we need to orient ourselves. We don't know what's happening behind us. If we can get to my SUV, we might get out of here alive."

She snorted. "My men are taking care of it. We will wait in the woods until I get the all-clear and then go back. Now move."

I shook my head. I had to stall her. The longer she was in control, the more dangerous the situation was. "We don't know who is waiting in the woods. There are professional killers out here after us, Sybil. Contract killers. My guess is that Hildago's regular men are engaging with yours and trying to flush us out where they will be out there, ready to ambush us. We're running in the wrong direction. We need to go back."

Her lips whispered in my ear, and I shivered. "You're trying to trick me again, aren't you?"

"What?" I turned to look at her, her green eyes

glinting in the darkness. "No, Sybil, I'm trying to *save* you. I'm trying to save us both."

An explosion sounded behind us and she jerked her head around in the direction it came from to see flames dancing from the roof of the barn. I pounced, grabbing the wrist of her hand that was holding the gun, and slammed it down on my knee to loosen her grip. The gun fell to the soft earth, and we fell together into the mud with her on top of me. She screamed and wrapped her hands around my throat, her eyes ablaze now with a wild fury. Just as I saw black spots clouding my vision, I brought my fists down hard on her forearms, breaking her grip, and as she sat back, I landed a punch in her face. She fell to the side with a cry of pain, and then it was a scramble to get to our feet as each of us landed blows. Someone had trained her decently well. Her punches were precise even in the dark-ness and the muck. We crashed into the cornstalks and just as I was able to roll away and get some distance; I heard the click of her safety and a snarl. "Get on your knees." I stilled.

"Sybil- "I whispered her name, but she cut me off.

"You could never just *listen* and do as you were told, Hannah. You always had to make things diffi-cult and *push* me to the breaking point." Her breathing was heavy, and her hands shaking. She was covered in mud and filth, her pretty mouth cut with blood trailing down her chin to her neck. "Maybe Sergei was right all along. Maybe it's time I let you go, finally." Her voice softened as she spoke her thoughts out loud.

"Sybil wait..." There was a soft click and then the world exploded around me. I watched in slow motion as her mouth formed a shocked O and blood bloomed from the center of her chest. I cried out, turning to see where the shot had come from, and lurched forward as I saw a dark shadow rising in the distance between a row of corn, the light from the burning barn glinting off the scope of his sniper rifle. Then a deep, burning pain registered in my chest and I looked down to see a matching bloom of crimson spreading across my shirt. The world twisted and suddenly I was staring into dark grey eyes that were bright with fear and worry. His mouth was moving, but I couldn't hear the words he was saying and then once more, everything went dark.

CHAPTER TWENTY-TWO

Hannah

Warmth spread over me and I sighed, snuggling deep into the cloud that seemed to be wrapped around me. Muffled sounds came to me: voices, laughter, seagulls calling, and the crashing of waves. Light penetrated my eyelids, and I squeezed them shut, willing myself to back into the dream. The sounds became louder, voices calling out to each other, children giggling. The waves sounded closer and less dream-like. I opened my eyes.

Pain. I winced softly as I attempted to sit up and then collapsed back down into a sea of down-filled pillows. Now I knew why I'd been dreaming about sleeping on a cloud. I looked around the room, confused. Where was I?

I slowly took in the room and wondered if I

wasn't still dreaming. Or maybe I was dead, and this was heaven. The room was large and looked like it belonged in some Grecian palace by the sea. Porcelain white columns with gilded decorations of birds and animals decorated the room. The floor was a shining marble and the bed I was in looked large enough to host an entire Olympic volleyball team. Large doors opened up to a balcony and an endless blue sky to my left. I looked to my right and saw a half-opened door that looked like it led to a bathroom or maybe a large walk-in closet.

There was a table next to my bed with a glass of water, some pills in a small cup, and a note. I picked it up and read. "Take your medicine. Drink your water. Clothes are in the armoire. Gun is in the drawer. I'll be back soon. - S."

More confused than ever, I set the note down and slowly tested out my feet on the marble floors. No dizziness, but I winced slightly at the way my muscles stretched and the sting of pain I felt in my chest. I looked down to see a small bandage covering a spot just to the right of my heart. Memories came back to me. Sybil, fighting in the mud, the barn burning brightly against the night sky. Then watching as Sybil pointed her gun and shot me. And Simon, holding me, telling me it would be okay.

I followed all the instructions but didn't take the pills. Something told me that my fuzziness and lack of recognition about what had happened over the past several days had something to do with the medicine. Instead, as I pulled the gun from the drawer and tucked it into the waistband of my yoga pants, I tossed the pills in the trash bin next to the side table and made my way to what I thought was the exit.

I found myself in a long hallway in what appeared to be a large mansion. Ok, so maybe not quite the palace that my drug-addled brain had thought it was, but it was still impressive. I passed room after room in the hall before I came to a set of stairs that wound down to what seemed to be the main floor. I'd yet to see one face and frowned. It was becoming unsettling. But then I remembered I'd heard voices and laughter coming from outside and searched for the way out.

I entered another room that looked like it might be a sitting area and saw large double doors similar to the ones in my room that opened out onto a grassy lawn. I stepped through the sunlight brighter here and squinted, trying to see if I could hear where the voices were coming from again.

"Hannah! You aren't supposed to be awake yet!"

A musical voice with a soft French accent reached me and I spun around.

"Rue!" The beautiful hacker was lounging on a chaise dressed in a neon blue bathing suit, her hair curled into twin buns on the side of her head and, for once, a book was in her hands, not a laptop.

"Where are we? How did I get here?" I approached and saw that just beyond her was a Grecian-style pool with a waterfall edge. And beyond the edge, an azure sky met with endless miles of deep blue ocean. I blinked in wonder.

Rue laughed and stood up to join me. "Beautiful isn't it? We're in Greece. Abrams decided our team needed some downtime before our next mission." She gave me a wink. "But I'm pretty sure Simon didn't give him a choice. He wasn't going to leave you again any time soon."

I looked around me, drinking in the beauty of the place. "Where is Simon?"

She turned back around and laid back down on the chaise, dropping her sunglasses back over her face. "He said he had to go take care of something, but that he'd be back. He thought you might wake up today and told me to stick around just in case."

I frowned at her. "Did you guys keep me drugged this entire time? How long have I been out?"

She shrugged and peered at me from over the top of her glasses. "A couple of weeks. To be fair, the doctors wouldn't have released you so early if Simon hadn't guaranteed them you would stay down and rested. You almost died, Hannah."

I turned around and looked at the view before me again. Children were flying kites and running up and down the white sandy beaches. Seagulls dipped and dived over the waves. The sun was shining and everything in me itched to run down to the sand to join them. Try as I might, I couldn't summon any outrage or indignation. He remembered.

"You'd said you always wanted to be near the ocean. So I brought you here." His rumbling voice and Scottish accent filled my ears, and I sighed, leaning back into him as powerful arms came around me.

"You killed my sister," I whispered softly, trying to understand the feelings that were swirling inside of me. Grief, guilt, and relief all at the same time.

"Aye." His lips nuzzled my jaw and shivered.

"I should kill you for it."

His teeth nipped at the junction of my neck and collarbone. "Aye, you should."

I turned around in his arms, looking up into those eyes that saw so much of me. That had seen me from the very first moment we'd met. "Thank you for coming for me."

He leaned down, his forehead pressed to mine, and his words rumbled through me straight to my heart. "I love you, Hannah Kelly. I'll always come for you." His lips brushed over mine tenderly, carefully.

I sighed against his lips, melting into the kiss, and then just as I was about to demand we head somewhere more private, Rue cleared her throat and called out.

"Sorry to interrupt, but we might need to cut our vacation short."

Simon pulled away and turned to her, glaring. But she wasn't paying attention and was standing, looking at a TV that was tucked into an alcove above a bar just off the side of the pool. A frazzled-looking reporter was on the news and behind him, people were running in chaos. The red bar across the screen flashed Breaking News, and the words made my heart still. "Dr. Death delivers warning to Western nations. Kills 25 in the terror-related attack."

Simon's phone rang, but I didn't pay attention as I inched closer to the screen. A picture flashed in the corner and I nearly fell to my knees. Sybil.

I heard Simon's voice through the static of my

thoughts. "It's not her, Hannah. Sybil is dead, I promise."

I nodded, still staring at the screen. "I know, but how?"

"It's a tactic to instill fear. They won't announce she's dead for a while. Or this was planned well before what happened at your parents. Abrams just called." He looked at me, his face unreadable, but I could tell by the set of his shoulders and the tense way he clenched his jaw that he hadn't liked the conversation.

"Let me guess, you have to go?" I almost choked on the words, my heart sinking.

He shook his head. "No. *We* have to go." He frowned down at me and took my hand. "If it's what you want. If not, tell me now and I'll tell Abrams to go feck off and let the world burn. But I won't do this without you, Hannah. Never again."

I stared at him and let his words sink in. "You mean Abrams gave me the thumbs up? To be on the team?" Simon just nodded, his thoughts still guarded.

A grin slowly spread across my face. "Well now, Mr. Gallagher. First, I think you owe me an apology."

He blinked in confusion and then stalked

towards me. "Tell me then, tell me what I need to apologize for and I'll do it, lass."

I cocked a hip and arched a brow. "Because I am *so* a Bond girl."

He stopped short and just stared at me for a moment. Then threw his head back and laughed so loud that Rue was startled and turned around to see what had happened. He swooped in the last few steps towards me and kissed me as if he was a man starved, then growled against my lips. "Aye, lass, but you're no Bond girl. You are so much better. You're mine."

ACKNOWLEDGMENTS

Holy cow I did it! I wrote an entire series. I couldn't have done it without the help of some amazing people and so I want to make sure I say thanks.

First, to my husband. You learning about this process, sharing in the ups and downs, encouraging me, and being supportive even when it was difficult to understand, has been amazing. Thank you for being you and loving me the way you do.

To my bestie-boo Debbie C. You are the Bad to my Moo. The Moo to my Bad. The best drum beater and encourager out there. I would not be here if it wasn't for you. THANK YOU.

To the Black Cat team and Andrea. Thank you for your support and wisdom and PATIENCE as I learned to navigate this world of being an author. You guys are amazing.

To Amelia H. Thank you for showing me how to broaden my horizons and giving me the tips and tricks I need to one day be successful in this world.

You are an amazing author and friend and I'm so blessed to know you.

To my beta-readers. You guys really helped me bring this story to life. Thank you for being there when I needed you and for having all the patience in the world with me. You are ROCK STARS.

And most importantly, to my readers and new fans. I can't thank you enough for the messages, reviews, and kind words. I have treasured each and every one of them. Thank you for everything.

-xoxo-

Anne

Anne Roman is a caffeine-fueled, multitasking mom and wife by day and the author of 'edge of your seat' romance books by night. She loves writing books that bring surprising twists, unexpected turns, and intense romance. When not writing you can find her playing Uber driver to her four children, having fun with her hunky husband, or staying up way past her bedtime to read.

You can join her mailing list and stay up to date on upcoming releases at www.anneromanauthor.com

Or follow her on any of her socials by searching for Anne Roman Author on TikTok, Facebook, or Instagram. She would LOVE to connect with you!